To Jen

BLACK TEARS

Gloria Williams

*Thanks So Much
for Supporting
me! Please keep
me and my book
journey in your
prayers !*

*Gloria Williams
5-16-17*

First Edition Design Publishing

Black Tears
Copyright ©2015 Gloria Williams

ISBN 978-1622-878-21-5 PRINT

LCCN 2015931488

February 2015

Published and Distributed by
First Edition Design Publishing, Inc.
P.O. Box 20217, Sarasota, FL 34276-3217
www.firsteditiondesignpublishing.com

Dedication

This book is dedicated to my late
parents, Mr. & Mrs. Theodore
Williams, and my late favorite
Uncle Sammy. I love and miss you!!

Acknowledgements

I would first like to thank God for blessing me with the gift to become a writer and published author. I also would like to thank my late mom for molding and shaping me into the person that I've become. Special thanks go out to my friends and family, for encouraging me during the lows and highs of this challenging period of my life. I also would like to give a special thanks to the editing crew at The Brain Surge Tutoring & Editing Company.

Prologue

Lorretta Lynn knew her life was getting ready to change as she watched the pall-bearers roll her favorite Great Aunt Edna's casket down the small church aisle. Tears rolling from her eyes, she's clinging to Grandma Hattie Mae. All she can think about is what's getting ready to happen to her life.

"Hi Sweetie," Mamie Lee says as she walks over and kisses Lorretta Lynn after the funeral.

"Oh, hi, Aunt Mamie Lee. How are you?"

"I'm doing pretty good, Sugah. How 'bout you?"

Lorretta Lynn doesn't say a word. Mamie Lee can tell by her facial expression that she is in a lot of pain. Mamie Lee reaches out her arms and grabs her niece around the neck. Lorretta Lynn drops her head and just starts sobbing . After a few minutes, Lorretta Lynn regains her composure and slightly pulls away.

"Oh, I forgot, you asked me how I was doing, didn't you?"

"Yes I did, but, Child, you ain't got to say a word. Baby, I know how you are feeling, because we all feel the same way."

Lorretta Lynn looks up with tears still embedded in her eyes, "I loved Aunt Edna so much. I just don't know if I can make it without her."

"Baby, I understand, but just remember that we all gon' be ok," Mamie Lee says, before looking over at Hattie Mae, who is only a few steps away.

"How are you holding on, Big Sister?"

"Lord, I'm just holding on ...just holding on. Sister had suffered for so long. I guess the Lord finally called her home. Lord, I'm sho' gon' miss her," She says, with tears forming in her eyes.

"Grandma?"

"Yes, Child?"

"You not gon' miss her more than me...I...I...just don't know why my Aunt Edna had to die," Lorretta Lynn says, before almost breaking down completely. The poor child is trying her best to hold it together.

"Baby, I know you are hurting, but death comes to all. ... None of us came here to stay," Hattie Mae says while Lorretta Lynn is wiping her eyes.

"Yeah, I know, Grandma. My Bible school teacher said that in class."

Mamie Lee opens the church door and notices all the people waiting in their cars.

"Come on y'all. Let's get out of this church. Lord, look at all the folks waiting in their cars with their lights on."

Mamie Lee walks out, and Lorretta Lynn and Hattie Mae follow behind her. All three look back at all the cars, and they start moving faster toward the limousine. Mamie Lee starts talking again, "Lord, we betta hurry up. Folks look like they are getting impatient."

Lorretta Lynn rushes even faster toward the family car, and Hattie Mae nods her head.

"Look like it's getting ready to rain," Mamie Lee says while climbing in.

"I sho' hope it don't rain 'til we at least leave the cemetery. I left my umbrella at home," Hattie Mae whispers.

Mr. Stone hears her comment and turns around from the steering wheel. "You don't have nothing to worry about, Madam. I have an umbrella that's big enough to cover everybody," He says, before turning around and clenching the driver's wheel.

"Thank you, Mister," Hattie Mae responds. Mr. Stone doesn't say a word, and the car is completely quiet now. He glances back to make sure everybody is stationary, and then he presses down on the accelerator. Off they go down the long country road. Tears are falling, and Lorretta Lynn is resting her tiny head on Aunt Mamie Lee's shoulder.

CHAPTER ONE

"Man, it's storming outside. How come it always have to storm when we don't have school?" Billy Ray says, as he's looking out the living room window. "I was really looking forward to playing outside today."

"Child, I don't reckon you will be playing outside today. It look like one of those days when it is going to rain all day," Hattie Mae says while rocking back in her rocking chair. Hattie Mae is knitting while she's talking to the kids.

"Grandma," Billy Ray says, while looking up at his grandmother with puppy dog eyes.

"Yes, Boy."

"How can you tell it's going to rain all day long?" He says, with a very disappointed look.

"Child, I can just tell. Don't you know Grandma been around long enough to predict the weather?"

"Oh...for real?"

"Yes, for real, Boy."

"I have another question then," He says, looking serious.

"What, Boy?"

"Since you know so much about the weather...why don't you just be a weatherman, Grandma?"

Lorretta Lynn and Debra Anne look at Billy Ray and burst out laughing. Hattie Mae knows Billy Ray is being sarcastic, so she grabs her belt from the side of the chair. Billy Ray's eyes get big as he watches her.

"Boy, hush your smart mouth. How in the world I'm gon' be a weatherman? You know I ain't got no education, and even if I did "They don't hire no color folks to be on T.V.," She says, while looking over at Billy Ray and rolling her eyes. She points her belt at Billy Ray, and he gets up quietly. He walks over to the other end of the living room table and bends down. Hattie Mae is watching his every move.

"Billy Ray!" She shouts out.

Billy Ray totally ignores her and continues looking inside the living room end table. She is really irritated now. She grabs her belt and screams at the top of her voice, "Boy, don't you hear me talking to you?!"

"Oh, yeah, Grandma, I heard you. I was just trying to find my playing cards. I apologize. I didn't mean to ignore you," He says, with a phony look on his face. Billy Ray really wasn't sorry. He purposely ignored Hattie Mae because she had threatened to hit him with her belt. Billy Ray turns around and looks at his big sister. "Do you want to play cards, Lorretta Lynn?" He says, while trying to switch the focus of the conversation.

"Oh, I don't care, Baby Brother. What do you want to play?" She says, while looking over at Hattie Mae.

"Oh, we can . . . play pity pat," He says before jumping up from the floor. "Do you want to play with us, Debra Anne?" He asks, patiently waiting for an answer.

"Naw, I don't want to play with y'all," She says, rolling her eyes at Lorretta Lynn.

"Oh, I forgot. I don't even know why I asked. You think you are too good to play with us," He says, before jumping due to the thunder and lightning. He quickly runs over and sits next to Lorretta Lynn. "Are you ready to play now?"

"I need to be asking if you're ready. You're running like you're scared," Lorretta Lynn says, while Billy Ray is shuffling the cards.

"I am scared. I don't want to be struck by lightning," He says, gazing at his big sister.

"Nah, we not gon' get struck by lightning. I think we are safe in the house. Come on--let's start playing."

Hattie Mae looks at the two kids while they are trying to find space on the floor. She's looking at Lorretta Lynn with a mean face, and Lorretta Lynn can tell she's getting ready to say something. Hattie Mae starts talking in an angry tone.

"How do you know we're safe in the house, Ms. Black Know-It-All?"

Lorretta Lynn looks over at Hattie Mae with a pitiful look. "Grandma, there you go calling me black again. Why do you always have to call me black?"

The sound of the poor girl's voice irritates Hattie Mae. She stands up and looks at Lorretta Lynn as if she could strangle her. She starts walking toward the kids, and Lorretta Lynn is getting nervous. Lorretta Lynn knows something is about to happen, but she can't figure it out in her head. Hattie Mae finally makes it to the kids and stares Lorretta Lynn up and down. Before Lorretta Lynn knows it, Hattie Mae is shouting at the top of her voice.

"I'm yo' grand mammy, and I can call you whatever I want to!"

She stands there, waiting for Lorretta Lynn to say something. She wants to pop her so bad that it's killing her. Lorretta Lynn remains quiet, as tears start forming.

"Do you hear me, Black Heffa?!"

"Yes, I hear you, Grandma," She says, while her voice is trembling.

Hattie Mae turns around and heads back to her rocking chair. Billy Ray is furious, and Debra Anne is sitting in the corner with a big smile on her face. Billy Ray anxiously waits for Hattie Mae to sit down. He then starts talking.

"Grandma?"

"What, Boy?"

"Why are you so mean to my big sister? You don't ever call Debra Anne out of her name," He says, anxiously waiting for an answer.

"Hush yo' mouth, Boy! You don't question me--I'm your grand mammy!"

Billy Ray doesn't say a word, and Lorretta Lynn knows better than to say anything. Lorretta Lynn starts dealing the cards, pretending that nothing ever happened. Hattie Mae grabs her yarn and starts knitting. The kids start playing cards, and Hattie Mae suddenly decides that this is a good time to tell her life story. She raises her head and starts talking.

"I been meaning to tell y'all my life story. It's still storming outside, so I may as well tell y'all now." She looks over at Debra Anne and says, "Go in the kitchen and get me some hot coffee before I start."

Debra Anne closes her journal. "Ok, Grandma, I'll go get you some coffee right now." She gets up from the couch and starts heading towards the kitchen.

"Hurry up, Child, so I can start my story. It's gon' take me a long time to tell y'all youngins about my life."

"Ok, Grandma," Debra Anne says before reaching for the hot coffee pot.

Billy Ray looks up from his card game and rolls his eyes while Hattie Mae is not watching. He drops his head again and starts focusing on the card game. "Ooh, I have a good hand this time, Big Sister."

Lorretta Lynn is getting ready to respond, until she's interrupted by Hattie Mae's shout. Both kids are wondering what's wrong with their grandmother. She shouts again, and they look at her like she's crazy.

"Oh, shit. Oh, shit!" Hattie Mae says, "I just saw that big damn cockroach again. Billy Ray, grab my house shoe over there and find that SOB!"

Billy Ray puts his cards down and stands up. He looks over at Hattie Mae before reaching for her house shoe. "What's a SOB, Grandma?"

Hattie Mae is irritated by his comment. She rises up from the rocking chair so fast that she almost knocks her coffee over. "Boy, what I tell you about asking so many questions? I ain't never seen no child that ask as many questions as you do." She snaps her house coat buttons and sits back down. Billy Ray just stares and starts talking again.

"Dang, Grandma, I only asked a simple question. My school teacher said it's a free country, and I can ask whatever I want to."

"Boy, ain't nobody stutting about what yo' school teacher said," Hattie Mae says, while sipping on her coffee. She spots the cockroach again. "There go that damn roach again--Lord, have mercy."

"I just saw it too, Grandma. It crawled underneath the refrigeration," Debra Anne says.

Billy Ray grabs his grandma's house shoe and starts heading towards the kitchen. "Man, I just saw it, and I missed the SOB!" He hollers out.

"Boy, what did you just say?" Hattie Mae says while grabbing her belt from the side of the chair.

"Oops, I'm sorry, Grandma. I meant to say cockroach," He says, praying Hattie Mae doesn't hit him. Hattie Mae knew Billy Ray said SOB on purpose. She jumps up so hard this time, her cocked-to-the-side wig almost fell off. The girls are trying not to laugh as she shakes her belt at Billy Ray, "Boy I got one more time to hear you repeat SOB, and I'm gon' whoop your tail 'til it rope like okra."

Billy Ray is wondering what 'rope like okra' means, but he refuses to say anything. Debra Anne decides to instigate the situation.

"Grandma,"

"Yes, Sweetie?"

"Billy Ray is lying. You should beat his tail, Grandma," She says, with a big smirk on her face. Debra Anne's comments make Billy Ray mad. He wants to pop her, but decides not to. She looks back over to Hattie Mae and starts talking.

"Grandma, can I get some graham crackers and milk?" Debra Anne asks, when Hattie Mae is enroute to the bathroom.

"Yes, go ahead, sweetie," Hattie Mae says, while closing the bathroom door.

"Shoot, I'm hungry too. I'm gon' ask Grandma if I can get some graham crackers and milk, too. Do you want some, Big Sister? I'm getting ready to ask right now," Billy Ray says, looking over at Lorretta Lynn.

"I want some. Go ahead and ask her," Lorretta Lynn says, suspecting that the answer is going to be no.

Billy Ray cups his hands around his mouth and looks toward the bathroom. "Grandma, can me and Big Sister get some graham crackers and milk, too?" He screams out.

"Naw, y'all ain't getting shit!" Hattie Mae screams through the bathroom door.

"What did you say, Grandma? I didn't hear you."

Lorretta Lynn had heard her loud and clear, but she refuses to bust Billy Ray's bubble. She stays silent while Billy Ray is waiting on an answer. Hattie Mae opens the bathroom door and shouts at the top of her voice.

"I said y'all ain't getting shit! Yo' mouth is too smart and your black-ass sister don't deserve any." Hattie Mae slams the door.

Lorretta Lynn's face literally drops down to the floor. Pain is almost becoming her best friend. She feels like striking back, but she fears the consequences. She immediately reflects back to how her Aunt Edna had always protected her. She drifts back from her thoughts when she hears Debra Anne in the kitchen, singing and smacking on her graham crackers. Billy Ray is annoyed by Debra Anne. He runs to the kitchen and throws a paper ball at her, then immediately runs back to the living room.

Debra Anne runs behind him, yelling, "You're just jealous because y'all can't have no graham crackers and milk. You betta be glad that paper ball didn't hit me, little punk!" Then she turns back around and heads back to the kitchen.

Hattie Mae is coming out the bathroom now. Billy Ray smells an odor and he immediately turns up his nose. Hattie Mae notices his facial expression and starts talking, "I don't care how much you frown, Boy, you still ain't getting' no graham crackers and milk."

Billy Ray looks her square in the face. "I'm not frowning about no stupid graham crackers. I'm frowning because something smell like a rotten egg and I didn't smell it until you opened up the bathroom door."

Hattie Mae is furious now. If looks could kill, Billy Ray would be dead. Lorretta Lynn is trying her best not to laugh. Debra Anne is laughing, because she knows nothing is going to happen to her. Hattie Mae walks over and grabs her belt off the chair. She points the belt at Billy Ray, with a look from Hell. She starts talking in a very angry tone.

"Boy, I'm so sick of your mouth. One day, I'm gon' get a hold of your tail and not let loose!"

Billy Ray is shaking and praying at the same time. He purposely said what he said because Hattie Mae wouldn't let them have any graham crackers and milk. Hattie Mae walks back over to her chair and sits down. Billy Ray is silently counting his blessings and smiling inside. Hattie Mae starts talking to Debra Anne.

"Debra Anne, bring me some more coffee when you come out that kitchen. Don't forget to put some cream and sugar in it this time."

"I will, Grandma, but the coffee has gotten a little cool."

"That's ok, bring it anyway," Hattie Mae says, noticing Billy Ray looking out the window. It's still pouring down raining, and the poor child is so disgusted. He walks back over to sit next to his big sister.

"Man, it's still raining outside. I'm mad!" He says, while Hattie Mae is looking over at him.

"Boy, didn't I tell you that it was going to rain all day long? You must think that I didn't know what I was talking about," She says, while Debra Anne is handing her some coffee.

"Don't spill your coffee, Grandma," Debra Anne says.

Billy Ray looks over at her and says, "You act like Grandma not used to holding coffee."

Hattie Mae ignores his comment and says, "Thank you, Sweetie."

Billy Ray and Lorretta Lynn just look at each other. They both are thinking the same thing. Hattie Mae always shows so much favoritism when it comes to Debra Anne.

Hattie Mae look up at the kids and start talking, "I want everyone to hush, because I'm getting ready to start my life story,"

Billy Ray looks over while she's sipping coffee. "Grandma, can I ask you one more question before you start your life story?" He's trying to stall.

"What, Boy? Hurry up."

"Why do we have so many roaches? We are clean. Me and Big Sister saw another one when you were in the bathroom."

Hattie Mae scratches her wig before looking over at Billy Ray. This is one time she doesn't get upset with him questioning her. She's just as sick of the critters as the kids are. "Child, I got these damn roaches when Justina gave me her dresser and chest of drawers. Momma always told me to be careful about taking folks' leftovers. I should have followed her instructions."

Billy Ray lets Hattie Mae finish talking, and then he started scratching his head. "Umm...Ms. Justina? Are you talking about the lady that come over here and she don't have no teeth in her mouth, Grandma?" He says, with a serious look on his face.

"Yes, Child...that's Ms. Justina."

"What happened to all her teeth, Grandma?"

"Child, when you get old, your teeth just start falling out. If you live long enough, you will see what I'm talking about," Hattie Mae says, while continuing to knit her blanket.

"Unt uh...I betcha my teeth not gon' fall out," He says, looking over at his Grandma.

"What make you think you gon' keep all your teeth, Boy?"

"'Cause, I'm gon' go to the dentist like my Uncle Bobby."

"Boy, it cost a lot of money to go to the dentist. You must plan on having a good paying job when you grow up," Debra Anne says from across the room.

"I am gon' have a good job, but I'm not gon' work on the railroad tracks like Uncle Bobby,"

"Where do you plan to work, Billy Ray?" Debra Anne says, eagerly waiting for an answer.

"Girl, I don't know. I'm just a kid. Why are you asking me a stupid question like that?"

"Well, you said you gon' make a lot of money. I thought you already knew what you want to be".

Billy Ray gives Debra Anne a disgusted look and then turns to Hattie Mae. Everybody knows he's getting ready to ask another question; he always gets a certain look before asking something he has no business asking. The room is silent and tense until he blurts out, "Grandma?"

"Yes, Boy?"

"I know you are getting ready to tell your life story, but I just need to tell you my idea first."

"Boy, what kind of idea do you have?" She asks, looking up at Billy Ray with her cat-eye glasses hanging below her nose.

"Well, I just thought about a good way to get rid of the roaches,"

"Boy, you still thinking about those damn roaches?"

"Yes, I am, Grandma, and here's my idea," He says, and the girls are wondering what's going to come out of his mouth.

"Go ahead, Boy, I'm listening, and you betta hurry up. I was supposed to start my story a long time ago."

"Ok, Grandma. Well, I was just thinking that we should let Ms. Justina come over and just sit in the kitchen for a while..."

"Boy, what on earth are you talking about?" Hattie Mae interrupts, "Why in the world do I need Ms. Justina to sit in my darn kitchen?"

Hattie Mae looks confused, and Billy Ray scratches his head while contemplating blurting out his idea.

"Well, I just think if she sit in the kitchen and smile...all the roaches will get scared and run away!"

Both girls bust out laughing, while Hattie Mae gets angry and reaches for her belt. Billy Ray doesn't move; he looks as innocent as a newborn baby.

Hattie Mae screams out from her rocking chair, "Boy, I ought to slap you! Hush yo' mouth! Don't you know, Ms. Justina can't help it that she don't have no teeth? You ought to be shame of yourself making a comment like that! Lord, I tell you the truth, I don't know where you get your smart mouth from. You must have gotten that shit from your Daddy's side of the family," Hattie Mae is rocking now; Billy Ray has struck another nerve, and the room becomes silent while he just humps up his shoulders. Billy Ray doesn't want to hear Hattie Mae's life story, so he tries to think of another distraction. Thankfully, the phone starts ringing.

"Grandma, can I please answer the phone this time?" He shouts out. Hattie Mae had gotten up and started walking back to her bedroom, and she is still fuming about how Billy Ray had talked about her friend's teeth.

"I just need a few moments of silence!" Hattie Mae shouts, before closing her bedroom door. Billy Ray calls her name again and she cracks open her bedroom door.

"Boy, let that damn phone ring! That probably ain't nobody but a bill collector. It's probably the insurance man, Mr. Roy. I was supposed to pay him last week," She says, before grabbing some more yarn off of her wooden dresser. She's been trying to finish knitting her neighbor's greatgrandbaby's blanket for the longest time. Once she picks up the yarn, she heads back to the living room.

Billy Ray hears her coming and starts talking, "Grandma, I hope you are getting ready to fix us something to eat. I'm starving, Grandma," He looks over at his big sister. Lorretta Lynn is reading a school book, and Debra Anne is writing in her journal.

Hattie Mae doesn't answer Billy Ray; she just walks over to the freezer. She pulls out some hotdogs and places them on the kitchen table. Then she grabs a can of pork and beans, and pours them into a lop-sided pot. She pulls a knife out of the kitchen tray and starts cutting up the hotdogs, then she drops them in the pot and heads back to the living room.

Billy Ray starts talking before she can sit down, "Grandma, did you put something on the stove?"

"What do you think I was in there doing, Boy?"

"Well, I asked you if you were getting ready to cook and you didn't say nothing."

"Well, you know everything else, I thought you knew what I was doing in the kitchen. Child, I ain't put nothing on that stove but some pork 'n' beans and weenies. Ain't much in there to cook. I gotta go to the market when I get my check."

"I'm glad you are cooking pork 'n' beans and weenies. That's one of my favorite meals, Grandma." He says, smiling from ear to ear.

"Good, then," Hattie Mae takes a seat in her rocking chair and starts knitting.

Lorretta Lynn is still reading, and Debra Anne is working a crossword puzzle now. Billy Ray is getting hyper, because he's been stuck in the house all day. He's jumping up and down, while Hattie Mae goes back to the kitchen. She knows the food is ready, because it doesn't take long for beans and hot dogs to cook. Hattie Mae starts humming Gospel songs while removing some plates from the kitchen cupboard. She fixes the plates and hollers out to the kids, "Y'all come on in here and eat!"

Billy Ray is the first person to respond. He jumps up and bolts to the kitchen. He is running so fast, someone would think he's getting ready to eat Thanksgiving dinner. The girls finally make it to the kitchen, and Billy Ray is already eating.

Debra Anne looks over at him with disgust, "Boy, you could have waited until we got in here. I bet you didn't even say your grace," She says, rolling her eyes. Billy Ray just ignores her and keeps on eating.

Hattie Mae becomes disgusted with his table etiquette, as usual. "Boy, why do you always act like you ain't ate in years? I ain't never in my life seen a child like you. Y'all hurry up and eat, so I can tell my life story," She says, while walking back to the living room.

Billy Ray is still smacking his lips, and says, "Y'all want some Kool-aid? I'm gon' ask Grandma if we can have some Kool-aid. Grandma!"

"Yes, Boy?"

"Can we have some orange Kool-aid? Remember, we only had water with dinner yesterday!" He shouts, standing up from the table.

"Go ahead, Boy, but you bet' not ask me for nothing else to drink today, do you hear me?"

"Yes, Grandma, I heard you. I won't ask for nothing else to drink today." He opens the refrigerator door and pulls out the Kool-aid. He closes the door and sets the Kool-aid on the table. He grabs three glasses from the counter and sets them on the table, then pours a jumbo glass and starts gulping it down. When he finishes drinking, he attempts to grab the pitcher again, but Debra Anne looks over at him and calls out Hattie Mae's name.

"What's wrong, Child?" Hattie Mae responds.

"Billy Ray just poured some more Kool-aid. Wasn't he supposed to ask you first?"

"I ain't getting ready to drink no more Kool-aid! I was just pouring this for tomorrow!" Billy Ray screams, while shooting Debra Anne the bird. He walks over and puts his cup in the refrigerator. He goes back to the living room and notices Hattie Mae reading the newspaper. He's praying that she has forgotten about telling her life story.

Hattie Mae looks up from her newspaper and starts talking, "I hope y'all chitlins are full,"

"Yes," They all say in unison.

"Well, I'm sho' glad, 'cause we ain't gon' have nothing else to eat but some spam sandwiches and fruit cocktails. Grandma is po', so we can't have big meals every day," She says, looking over her glasses.

"How come we are so poor, Grandma?" Billy Ray asks, while pushing one of his trucks across the living room floor.

"Child, I don't get a lot of money to live on. Grandma is on a fixed income."

"What's a fixed income, Grandma?" He looks up from the floor.

"Boy, a fixed income mean my money is short, and don't ask me no more questions today! Lord, I get so tired of your mouth," She says, with a disgusted expression.

Billy Ray just looks at his Grandma blankly. *I'll ask you another question if I want to. I don't want to hear your stupid life story, anyway,* he's thinking.

"Well, y'all full, now. I can finally start my life story," Hattie Mae says, looking around the room.

"Grandma," Billy Ray says, trying to stall time.

"What now, Boy?"

"Can I go to the bathroom before you start your life story?"

"Go ahead, Boy, but you betta hurry up and get your butt back in this living room."

"Ok, I hear you. It won't take me long," He darts down the small hallway enroute to the bathroom. Billy Ray has no intentions on coming back anytime soon. He had placed his small toy boat in his pants' pocket earlier. He makes it to the bathroom and closes the door, then he turns the face bowl water on and plugs the sink. He starts playing with his toy boat in the water until he is interrupted by Hattie Mae's voice.

"Billy Ray!"

"Huh?" He screams out, surprised.

"Boy, what on earth are you doing in that bathroom? It don't take a hundred-year-old man this long to use the bathroom!"

"Oh, I'm doing number two, but I'm getting ready to come right now," He says, while flushing the toilet as if he had used it.

"I'm gon' number two your tail if you don't hurry up and get back in here!" She exclaims, gazing over at the belt that is lying under the living room table.

"Ok, here I come, here I come," He says, letting the water out of the sink and placing the wet boat in his pocket. He opens the door and rushes back to the living room. He dives onto the couch as if he's jumping in a pool. Debra Anne notices that his pants' pocket is wet.

"Billy Ray, how come your pants' pocket is wet?" She asks innocently, looking over at him.

Billy Ray and Lorretta Lynn know she is trying to get him in trouble. He looks at her with a puzzled expression, "Oh, I accidentally got some water on my pocket when I was washing my hands. Dang, it's still raining outside," He's trying to shift the conversation, "You said it was going to rain all day, Grandma. I guess you were right."

"Yes, Lord, I told you that. Boy, you betta stop complaining about the Lord's work. God made the rain and the sun. It can't be sunny all the time. Don't you know, the rain is what makes the plants and vegetables grow?" She says, while the kids are looking at her with 'whatever' looks. "Well, let me start my life story now. I'm gon' tell y'all about y'all's Momma first."

"Ok," Billy Ray says. Lorretta Lynn and Debra Anne are quiet.

"Y'all's Momma got pregnant when she was a senior in high school. She start messing around with a smut-black boy name Gus, and got pregnant with you, Lorretta Lynn. That's why you turned out so black and ugly," She says, looking over at Lorretta Lynn.

"Grandma!" Billy Ray shouts as he notices pain on Lorretta Lynn's face.

"What, Boy?" Hattie Mae looks down at her yarn.

"That was mean, what you just said about my big sister. I thought you 'posed to be a Christian, Grandma!" He says, moving closer to Lorretta Lynn, who is crying. He picks up some tissue from the end table and wipes his sister's eyes.

Hattie Mae stares at both kids like they're crazy, then starts knitting and talking again, "What you mean, what I said was mean? The truth is just the truth, and I bet' not hear you say nothing else about me pretending to be a Christian. Do you hear me, Boy?"

"Uh huh, I heard you," He says, rolling his eyes when she turns her head. Both Billy Ray and Loretta Lynn are getting to the point where they almost despise their grandmother. Hattie Mae looks over and notices tears falling from Lorretta Lynn's eyes.

"Girl, what you sitting over there crying for? I can't help it that yo' Momma had you by a black, ugly nigga."

Billy Ray's heart rate jumps up and he's fuming now. Lorretta Lynn starts crying harder, and it's taking everything for her not to lash out. Billy Ray tries to calm down as he embraces his sister. He pecks her on the cheek, while Debra Anne looks at them with a big smirk on her face. He's very angry, and decides to jump up from the couch.

"Boy, what you getting up for? Sit your tail down, so I can finish telling my story. I don't know why you're getting so upset. You should be clapping that yo' Momma didn't have *you* by no black, ugly nigga."

Billy Ray remains standing, and he's looking at Hattie Mae as if he could strangle her. He reaches into his pocket and pulls out his toy boat, then he throws the boat against the wall at full force. The boat hits the wall so hard, it ricochets back near Hattie Mae's head. Hattie Mae jumps up from the chair in an attempt to avoid the flying boat. She's in a blind rage, and almost stumbles and falls.

"Sit down, Boy! Sit down right now!" Hattie Mae screams at the top of her lungs, "I should beat the living crap out of you for almost hitting me with that damn boat!"

"I sho' wish it woulda..." Billy Ray mumbles, taking a seat on the couch next to Lorretta Lynn.

"What you say, Boy?" Hattie Mae demands.

"Nothing," He says, with his lips poked out. He is silently wishing that the boat had hit her. The room is quiet now. Tears are rolling from Lorretta Lynn's eyes and Billy Ray is looking sad. Debra Anne is in another world, as usual. She couldn't care less about what went on between her Grandma and her siblings.

While the house is still quiet, Hattie Mae decides to get up and walk to the kitchen. She grabs the coffee off of the stove and pours a fresh cup. Lorretta Lynn takes advantage of her absence, and tip toes to her room. Hattie Mae returns to the living room shortly after, and notices that Lorretta Lynn is gone.

"Boy, where did your black ugly sister go? You betta go get her before I beat her back to this living room!"

Billy Ray doesn't say anything. He looks at Hattie Mae, then jumps up from the couch. When he gets to Lorretta Lynn's room, he notices that she's laying in the bed, crying and clenching their Momma's Bible. He gently walks over to her bed and sits directly by her head. He bends down and places his tiny arm around her neck.

"Don't cry, Big Sister," He says in a low tone, "Everything is going to be alright. Remember, Mommy is in heaven with God, and they're both watching over us." He takes his tiny hand and starts wiping her eyes before Hattie Mae begins hollering.

"What are y'all doing back there? Y'all betta hurry up and get back in here. Y'all gon' make me come back there and tear y'all's tails up!"

"Ok! We're coming right now!" Billy Ray screams back, with anger in his voice, "Come on, Big Sister. Let's go finish listening to Grandma's life story before we get a whipping."

"Yeah, you are right, Baby Brother. Thanks for coming back here and checking on me. I love you so much," Lorretta Lynn says, before struggling to walk back to the war zone.

"I love you, too, Big Sister."

The two make it back to the living room, and Debra Anne is sitting in a chair, writing in her journal. Hattie Mae is staring and waiting for them to sit down.

"I don't want nobody else to get up and leave this room. Do y'all chitlins understand me?" She says, glaring over her cat-eye glasses.

"Yes, Grandma," they all say in unison.

Hattie Mae takes a sip from her coffee and repositions herself in her rocking chair. She straightens her big house coat and starts talking again, "Lord, I done forgot where I stopped my story. Lord, have mercy," She says, scratching her lop-sided wig. She pauses to recollect, then starts back up, "That old black nigga Cookie was fooling around with was a popular singer. Everybody in town kept saying his folks had a lot of money. I guess that's why the old bastard thought he could get a pretty girl like Cookie. Cookie was real light-skinned, and she had real long, pretty hair. That's where you got your good looks from, Debra Anne."

Lorretta Lynn and Billy Ray just listen. Debra Anne is sitting in the corner, blushing and gazing at her siblings. Lorretta Lynn planned to stay quiet, but she decides to speak up this time. She's tired of her Grandma talking about her Daddy. She looks over at Hattie Mae with pain on her face.

"Grandma?"

"What!"

"Please don't call my Daddy a bastard again," Lorretta Lynn says, fighting back tears.

Hattie Mae raises up from her chair with a look from Hell. She starts walking toward Lorretta Lynn, and the kids can tell something is about to happen. Lorretta Lynn and Billy Ray both are praying silently. Hattie Mae is almost in front of Lorretta Lynn's face, when Billy Ray decides to shout.

"Grandma! Grandma! Please don't do nothing to my big sister. She didn't mean to make you mad," He jumps in front of his sister, trying to protect her.

Hattie Mae glares at him. She suddenly shoves him and says, "Get out my way, Boy! Move it, right now!"

Billy Ray reluctantly eases away and Lorretta Lynn is looking like she's seen a ghost. She's trembling and praying silently. Hattie Mae reaches her arm out and pinches the poor girl's nose as hard as she can. Lorretta Lynn is squirming until Hattie Mae finally lets go of her nose.

"Let me tell you one thing, you black, ugly heffa! Don't you ever tell me what to say in my house! How many times I done told you that I'm yo' Grandmammy? If I want to call your smut-black, dead Daddy a bastard, umpteen times a day, I will! Do you hear me?" Hattie Mae growls, with her fist balled.

"Yes, yes, Grandma...I hear you..." Lorretta Lynn says, shaking like a leaf on a tree. She's silently thanking God that Hattie Mae didn't hit her with her fist. Hattie Mae stands there for a few minutes, and then heads back to her rocking chair. Billy Ray shoots her a bird while she's walking. She reaches over for her cold coffee and starts talking again.

"Y'all two damn worsen kids been disturbing me all day long. It done got late, and I know y'all think I'm not gon' finish my story. I'm gon' make a lie out of both of y'all. Y'all's butts gon' sit here 'til I finish, and I dare y'all to get up again."

The room is quiet as a mouse. Both kids refuse to challenge Hattie Mae anymore today. They are thinking about how they hate their Grandma's mean ways. Hattie Mae interrupts their thoughts to start telling her story again.

"All the folks in town kept saying smut Gus was on dope. Sho' 'nuff, one cold day they found him stretched out in an alley with a needle stuck in his arm. Smut Gus died from a drug overdose."

The room has become very, very quiet. Lorretta Lynn had often wondered what had happened to her Dad. Now she knows. She immediately starts visualizing her Dad stretched out in an alley. *Lord, have mercy...Lord, have mercy*, are her inner thoughts. Billy Ray breaks the silence.

"Grandma?" He says, looking over at Hattie Mae.

"Yes, Boy?"

"Are you finished now? Can we go to our rooms?" He is jumping up before Hattie Mae can answer him. He starts skipping down the hall, but stops in his tracks when he hears Hattie Mae call his name.

"Boy, I wasn't finished yet. I was getting ready to tell y'all about your Daddy's skunky folks."

Billy Ray starts skipping backwards when he hears Hattie Mae say 'Daddy'. He makes it back to the living room and sits down. Even though he's very young, he's still very curious as to what had happened to his Dad. This is the only time he's been anxious to hear the rest of Hattie Mae's story.

"Grandma?"

"Yes, Boy, and what I tell you about leaving this room?"

"Oh, I thought you were finished. But anyway, Grandma,"

"Anyway what?"

"I have a question. Did you say my Daddy's folks smelled like skunks? I sure hope my daddy didn't smell like a skunk. Skunks really stink," He says, while both girls burst out laughing.

"What y'all laughing for? Skunks do stink," Billy Ray says, with a serious look on his face.

Hattie Mae is just shaking her head and Lorretta Lynn is finally out of her funk. It's rare that she even feels like laughing. She often thanks God for Billy Ray, because in the midst of all of her challenges, Billy Ray can put a smile on her face. Her silent thoughts are interrupted by Hattie Mae.

"Boy, why on earth do you always have to twist stuff around? Lord, have mercy, I ain't never seen no child like you," She says, shaking her head again.

"What are you talking about, Grandma?" He says, eagerly waiting for an answer.

"Boy, I said skunky, but I didn't mean that yo' Daddy's folks stunk."

"Well, what did you mean, Grandma? One day, I smelled a bad odor when I was with Uncle Bobby, and he said it was a skunk."

"Boy, just forget I ever said that, ok? Lord, have mercy, Jesus," She says, straightening her crooked wig again. "Go to the kitchen and get me some fresh coffee."

"Grandma, it's late. You still want some coffee?" He asks, getting up from the couch.

"Boy, it ain't never too late for me to drink coffee."

She waits patiently for Billy Ray to fix her coffee. She picks up the newspaper from the coffee table and starts reading. Hattie Mae is looking at the obituaries when she suddenly hears racket coming from the kitchen. She knows Billy Ray has broken something, but she's not sure what it is. She looks up from the newspaper and hollers out to the kitchen.

"Boy, what on earth are you doing in that kitchen? Sound like you done broke something."

"Oh, Grandma, you not gon' believe what I just broke! I'm sorry!"

"What do you mean, you are sorry?"

"Oh...I just broke your favorite coffee cup."

"What do you mean, you broke my favorite cup? Don't you know that cup came from someone special? Lord, have mercy. I tell you the truth, y'all two kids gon' kill me."

Hattie Mae doesn't know that Billy Ray is smiling, because he broke the cup on purpose. He knew it was her favorite cup, but he didn't know which special person had given it to her. He pulls the broom out and starts sweeping the floor.

Hattie Mae screams out from the living room, "Boy, fix me another cup of coffee and get yo' tail back in here!"

"Ok, Grandma, I will be in there in a few minutes." Billy Ray takes another cup out and sets it on the counter. "Do you want a lot of cream and sugar this time, Grandma? I know some time you like your coffee black," He says, trying to butter up Hattie Mae.

"Yes, Boy, put me some cream and sugar in it."

"Ok, I will be in there in a few minutes." He fixes the coffee and pastes a serious look on his face. He tip toes back, pretending like he's being extremely careful. He hands Hattie Mae the coffee and sits next to Lorretta Lynn.

"Grandma?"

"Yes, Boy?"

"Did you say somebody special gave you that cup?"

"Yes, that's exactly what I said."

"Was it your boyfriend or somebody? 'Cause I ain't never seen no man come over here to see you. Oh, I forgot...the fruit man come over here sometimes. Don't all ladies supposed to have a boyfriend or husband, Grandma?"

"Boy, stay out of grown folks' business. Your tail is too grown. You ain't got no business worrying about me and a man," She acts like she's getting ready to pop him playfully, and he just smiles.

"Grandma?"

"What do you want this time, Boy?"

"I just have one more question,"

"Yes, Boy?"

"What ever happened to *my* Daddy?"

Hattie Mae pauses after Billy Ray's question. As much as she had stressed telling her life story, she really wasn't ready to talk about what had happened to Billy Joe. All of the kids are waiting anxiously to hear what she's going to say. She drifts back from her sad thoughts and starts talking again.

"Well, let me tell you what happened to your Daddy. It done got really late, but I'm gon' go ahead and tell y'all tonight," She pauses while painful memories cloud her mind; she's praying silently to God, asking for strength to tell the story, "All I can tell you, is that yo' daddy was a real light-skinned man, and a lot of folks thought he was white. Folks said he was so light because he was a product of slavery."

"Ok. But, I still want to know what happened to my Daddy?" Billy Ray says, looking more serious than he's ever looked, "Also, I don't know what slavery is, Grandma. Can you please tell me what a slavery is, after you tell me what happened to my Daddy?"

"Boy, why do you have to ask so many questions?" Debra Anne says, twirling her long ponytail. She's tired and very ready to go to bed. She gives Billy Ray a mean look, "Can you please just let Grandma finish her story without any more interruptions?"

"Shut up, you yellow banana," He says, rolling his eyes.

"Y'all chitlins hush. Boy, I'm gon' go ahead and tell you what a slave is, and what slavery mean," Hattie Mae says, stalling.

"Ok, I'm listening."

"Child, a slave is somebody that have to do whatever their slave master tell them to do. Sometimes slaves got beat, because they didn't obey their slave masters."

"For real, Grandma?" Billy Ray says, with a puzzled look.

"Yes, for real. People went through a whole lot back in slavery days," She says, looking at the blanket that she had almost finished. All eyes are on her, but Billy Ray starts talking again.

"Grandma?"

"Yes, Boy?"

"Are me and Lorretta Lynn slaves?"

Hattie Mae looks over at Billy Ray with a confused look. She's trying to figure out what had made him say what he just said. She puts the needle and yarn down.

"Boy, what on earth are you talking about?"

"Well, you beat me and Big Sister when we don't behave, so we must be slaves, too," He says, looking as serious as a heart attack.

Hattie Mae is furious. She throws her yarn and needle down and jumps up so fast she almost loses her balance. Both girls are trying their best not to bust out laughing. Hattie Mae puts her right hand on her hip, and the other hand in a fist position. She shakes her fist at Billy Ray and starts screaming at the top of her voice.

"Boy, let me tell you one thing! As long as you live, don't you ever make a comment like that! Did you hear what I just said, Boy? Next time you say something like that, I'm gon' knock the living daylight out of you!" She's fuming, and Billy Ray and the girls have never seen her this angry; all of their smiles disappear.

Hattie Mae is so upset she start walking toward her room, mumbling, "Lord, that boy get on my nerves. I got to go to the bathroom and get me some aspirins. Lord, have mercy, Lord have mercy…"

Pain rushes all over her body. Talking about slavery had brought back a lot of bad memories, ones she never cared to think about. Tears are falling from her eyes as she grabs her aspirin out of the bathroom medicine cabinet. She pours the aspirin in her hand and heads back to the kitchen.

Lorretta Lynn is whispering under her breath, "Boy, you shouldn't have said that. You betta apologize to Grandma when she get back in the living room."

Billy Ray is looking as if he hadn't said a word. In his little mind, he can't comprehend the difference. He starts whispering back to Lorretta Lynn, "But, Big Sister, she does beat…" He tries to get the words out, but Lorretta Lynn covers his mouth.

Hattie Mae is still in the kitchen, gulping down her aspirin. When she finally makes it back to the living room, Billy Ray and the kids are waiting patiently. Lorretta Lynn is thinking about what just happened. She can't believe that she actually feels bad that Billy Ray upset her Grandmother. In spite of how badly Hattie Mae treats her, Lorretta Lynn still loves her Grandma. She knows, deep down inside, that Hattie Mae could have given her away. She drifts back from her thoughts when she hears Billy Ray's voice.

"Grandma," He says softly,

Hattie Mae doesn't answer, and Billy Ray just waits. A few seconds pass, and he calls her name again. She finally looks up, with pain still on her face, "Yes, Boy?"

"I'm sorry for saying that...will you accept my apology?" Billy Ray asks, with puppy dog eyes.

"Yes...I reckon," She answers, remembering that Billy Ray is only a child.

Billy Ray really feels bad, because his big sister has confronted him. He doesn't mind sassing Hattie Mae, but he never wants to disappoint Lorretta Lynn. Everybody is quiet, and surprisingly enough, he shifts the conversation back to Hattie Mae's life story.

"Grandma, can you tell me now what happened to my Daddy? You never did get to that part."

Hattie Mae is calm now, and she's glad that Billy Ray has changed the subject. She looks over at him and starts talking again, "Baby, one day yo' daddy went fishing with some white friends, and he never returned home. Billy Joe's friends said he drowned, but no one ever found out the true story," She says, while tears are forming in her eyes.

"Grandma," Debra Anne says from across the room,

"Yes, Sweetie?"

"Is that when our Mommy started taking pills?"

"Yes, Lord. Y'all's Momma started taking pills and drinking a lot of alcohol. One day, I was waiting on y'all's Momma to come over and she never showed up. I got so worried, whereas I got on the phone and called a cab. I went over there and I kept knocking on y'all's door. I knocked and knocked, and she never came. I knew she was supposed to be in the house, 'cause I heard the record player playing. I was so worried, I asked the cab driver to call the police. The police came right away, and he had to force himself into the house. Lord, he opened the door, and my child was lying dead on the floor. Cookie had died from a drug overdose,"

Hattie Mae says, and tears are forming in everybody's eyes, "Lord, have mercy. I will never forget that day."

They are all crying now, and Billy Ray scoots closer to his big sister. Debra Anne gets out of her chair and walks over to sit next to Billy Ray. All of the kids are hugging and Hattie Mae is speechless. She grabs her Bible off of the end table and opens it to Psalms.

Billy Ray can't stand the tension anymore. He suddenly breaks away from both of his sisters and jumps off the couch, "I'm going to the kitchen and get me some ice cream and cookies!" He dashes to the kitchen while tears are still embedded in everybody's eyes.

CHAPTER TWO

"Can we eat now?" Billy Ray says, while shoving some cornbread in his mouth.

"Boy, please, you been eating ever since Grandma and Aunt Mamie Lee sat the food on the table," Debra Anne says, looking over at her baby brother.

Billy Ray doesn't pause from eating, he just keeps smacking his lips and shrugs his shoulders. Uncle Buck decides to join in on the conversation.

"Boy, I see why you are smacking. Hattie Mae and Mamie Lee put their foot in this food. Lord, this food is good," He says, licking his fingers, which are covered with collard greens juice. Billy Ray notices him licking and starts talking with a mouth full of food.

"Oooh, Uncle Buck, you are licking your fingers at the table. Grandma said that's bad table manners! She almost whooped me for doing that," Billy Ray says, while still smacking his lips. He is waiting on Buck to answer, when Hattie Mae suddenly butts in.

"Boy, what I tell you about flopping your mouth so much?" She is looking frustrated, and is getting ready to say something else, but Buck interrupts.

"Sister, I ain't paying that boy no mind. You know I'm a country boy, and this is how we eat in the country. Don't nobody use no fork when they're eating collard greens and hot water bread," He says, before biting into his fried chicken leg.

"Yeah, you sho' is right, Buck. A lot folks do eat with their fingers in the country. I'm just trying to teach these chitlins some good table manners. I would hate for them to be eating with their fingers, up at that school with those white folks," She says, while gazing at her grandkids. She takes another bite of greens and looks over at Mamie Lee, "Little

Sister, what did you put in these greens? I'm like Buck...they sho' taste good."

"Child, I ain't put nothing in those greens but some big old ham hocks, red peppers, onions and salt."

"Well, I'm sho' gon' try your recipe. I ain't had no greens that taste like this in a long time."

Everybody is talking and enjoying their food, when Lorretta Lynn accidentally belches. She immediately excuses herself, but that's not good enough for Hattie Mae. Hattie Mae suddenly jumps up, and the whole table gets quiet. They know she is getting ready to go into a rage, and everybody tries to brace themselves. Hattie Mae reaches into the kitchen drawer and starts pulling out her long, thick, black leather belt. Fear flashes across Lorretta Lynn's face, as Hattie Mae moves closer to her with the belt. Hattie Mae starts screaming at the top of her voice.

"Get yo' black ass up from this table! Get up right now!" She shouts, as the poor girl starts trying to get out of her seat. Loretta Lynn's not moving fast enough, and Hattie Mae is getting angrier and angrier. Loretta Lynn is stumbling while trying to push her chair into the table.

"What's taking you so long, you black heffa?"

"But, Grandma...." Loretta Lynn stammers.

"Don't 'but' me! Get yo' black tail out of this kitchen! You ain't nothing but a disgrace to this family!" Hattie Mae is still screaming, and Lorretta Lynn is rushing now. The poor child almost falls as she's trying to make it out of the kitchen.

All eyes are on Hattie Mae, and Billy Ray and Mamie Lee are fuming. Lorretta Lynn mumbles, "I am sorry" as she's walking, and that really sets Hattie Mae off. She hauls off and pops her as hard as she can with the belt. Lorretta Lynn is crying and running, and Hattie Mae rushes behind her and pops her again.

Mamie Lee is furious now. She jumps up from the table and hurries after her sister. Billy Ray starts screaming and throws his plate on the floor. Buck and Debra Anne are still sitting at the table, speechless.

Mamie Lee is shouting, "You're going to Hell! You're going to Hell!", as she rushes back to the kitchen and grabs her purse. She pulls Buck up from the table and they dash out the door. Billy Ray is in a frenzy, and Lorretta Lynn is now locked in her room. She falls on her knees and starts praying to God.

Billy Ray flies to his room and slams the door. "Somebody please help us, God! Somebody please help us!"

A couple of hours have passed, everyone is in their rooms, and the house is completely quiet. Hattie Mae creeps out of her room and walks toward the kitchen. She pulls the coffee pot out of the cupboard and starts making some coffee. Billy Ray has jumped out of bed and he's pacing his bedroom floor. He looks over in the corner and notices his teddy bear. He walks over and grabs it, then suddenly slams it on the bed. A moment later, he picks his bear back up and holds him in his arms. He's in deep thought, and he's yearning to confront Hattie Mae. Billy Ray loves his big sister, and often feels like it is his responsibility to protect her. He has to confront his Grandma, and he has to do it right now. He finally opens up his bedroom door and starts making his way down the tiny hall. Tears are still embedded in his eyes as he makes it to the kitchen. He notices Hattie Mae bending over, washing dinner dishes. She is humming Gospel songs when she turns around and sees him standing there.

"Boy, I didn't even know you were standing there. What's wrong with you?" She says, placing the dish rag on the kitchen counter.

Billy Ray doesn't say a word. He's searching his little mind for the right things to say. He's smart enough to know that he has to use a certain choice of words when mentioning anything related to Lorretta Lynn. He's been crying so much, his poor little nose is running. Little by little, he's building his strength up to confront his Grandma.

Hattie Mae notices his nose running, and she reaches over for a napkin. She starts wiping his nose, and tears are still falling from his little puppy dog eyes. "Boy, why you crying? Did you have a bad dream or something?"

"No, Grandma, I didn't have no bad dream. I'm sad, because you are so mean to my big sister," He says, wiping the tears from his eyes.

Hattie Mae is speechless, as she stares directly into her Grandson's face. This is the first time that she has actually felt his pain and wanted to do something about it. She rinses a few dishes and walks away from the sink. Then, she grabs Billy Ray's tiny hand and starts leading him toward the living room. They take a seat on the couch, and she straightens her big housedress, stamped with pins all over. Hattie Mae looks at Billy Ray with pity. Billy Ray is dying to hear what she's getting ready to say. She pauses for a minute to sip her coffee, then she places the cup down and starts talking.

"Baby, let me tell you something that you might not want to hear. I know it may seem that I am acting mean sometimes, but Grandma is just trying to raise y'all chitlins to grow up and be somebody. Lorretta Lynn is so black, whereas I have to work extra hard with her. She still might not be able to get no job doing nothing but scrubbing some rich white folks' floors. You see, real dark-skin folks have a harder time trying to make it in this world. Baby, you don't understand now, but when you grow up you'll see what Grandma is talking about."

Billy Ray is just looking at his Grandma. He's trying to make sense of what she just said. All he knows right now is that he loves his big sister, and he's tired of Hattie Mae mistreating her. Hattie Mae is watching him, and he's still just staring. She can tell he's confused, but she doesn't know any other way to explain her point of view. She didn't have the heart to tell him that she despises his big sister, and often thinks of Lorretta Lynn as a black curse on the family. Hattie Mae drifts back from her thoughts, while Billy Ray is still in a trance. She disrupts his mood to say, "Do you have any more questions for Grandma?"

He looks at her with sad eyes, "No. I'm getting ready to go back to my room now."

Billy Ray gets up from the couch and walks back to his room. He is glad that he confronted her. He doesn't feel any better, but at least he tried to do something. He closes his bedroom door behind him.

Hattie Mae walks back to the kitchen and starts running some fresh dish water. Lorretta Lynn is still in her room, but she's been standing by her door, eavesdropping on the whole conversation. Hattie Mae's comments about dark-skinned people are ringing in her mind. *Lord...Lord...Lord...*are her only thoughts.

The Next Day
Knock...knock...knock...

"Who's knockin'?" Hattie Mae screams from the kitchen area.

"It's your baby brother, Bobby B. Let me in!" He hollers from the other side of the door.

Hattie Mae fastens her housedress and heads toward the living room door. When she unlocks it, Bobby B is standing there, wearing a big smile. Hattie Mae's just as happy to see him as he is to see her.

"Come on in, Bobby B. Lord, we ain't seen each other in ages," She says, while greeting him with a big kiss.

"Lord, you are right, Big Sister. I been so busy working at the railroad, whereas I hadn't had a chance to make it over to see you and the chitlins. Where are my little babies anyway?" He asks, looking down the hallway toward their rooms. As soon as he says that, Billy Ray comes flying down the hallway, running so fast, he almost falls.

"Watch it, Boy, watch it, Boy," Bobby B says, while holding his large arms out.

"Uncle Bobby, Uncle Bobby! Give me five!" Billy Ray says, while greeting his uncle with his little hand in a high-five position. Bobby B spreads his large hand out and places it on Billy Ray's tiny hand. The two slap each other's hands, and they are grinning from ear to ear.

Billy Ray is staring his uncle up and down. Bobby B is wearing the cowboy hat that is Billy Ray's favorite. Billy Ray is looking at his hat and smiling.

"Uncle Bobby, you are wearing my favorite cowboy hat. Will you buy me a hat like that?" He asks, while the girls make it to the living room. Hattie Mae overhears Billy Ray asking Bobby B to buy him a hat, and she calls out from the kitchen.

"Boy, what I tell you about always begging your Uncle Bobby? He can't hardly get in the door without you begging him," She says, while both girls are jumping for joy at Bobby B's presence.

"Uncle Bobby! Uncle Bobby!" Lorretta Lynn cheers.

"Come on over here, Sugah, and give me a big hug. How's my big baby girl doing?" Bobby B says, spreading his arms out again. Lorretta Lynn gives him a big bear hug. She didn't want to answer his question, because she would reflect back to how she was feeling about her Grandma's predictions for her future. Bobby B smacks her on the cheek, and she giggles and flinches, because his sharp whiskers tickle.

Billy Ray is getting jealous, and he wants some more attention. He takes his little body and scoots between his big sister and Bobby B. Debra Anne is just standing and staring. Bobby B motions to her, "Come over here, too, I have enough hugs for everybody," He says, and she moves closer to give him a hug.

"How are you doing, Uncle Bobby?" Debra Anne asks, smiling.

"I'm doing good, Sugah, just a little tired. I been standing up at the railroad all day. It feels good, sitting here resting these old bones," He says, while the kids giggle at his comment. Bobby B calls out to Hattie Mae, who is standing down the hall, "Big Sister, what are you doing down that hall? Come on back in here with me and these chitlins."

"I'm coming, Baby Brother. I'm just down here, watering my plants. I forgot I hadn't watered them in a few days. I didn't think about watering them until I saw you...probably 'cause you bought me the biggest one that I have."

"Child, you still got the plant that I bought you for Mother's Day?"

"Yes, sir. You know I have a green thumb. My plants last a long time. I'm the only person in town that can make a dead person's plant live a long time. You know, the old folks said dead folks' plants don't live a long time," Hattie Mae muses, heading back to the living room.

"Sho' 'nuff," Bobby B says.

"What is Billy Ray running his mouth about now?" Hattie Mae says, looking over at him.

"He's just fussing with his big sister. You know he don't want nobody getting more attention than him," Bobby B chuckles, while pecking Billy Ray on the cheek again.

Billy Ray starts looking down at his pockets, "Uncle Bobby, do you have any money in your pockets?"

Hattie Mae is annoyed by that question, "Boy, what I tell you about begging your Uncle Bobby all the time? Lord, you are one of the most begging kid that I have ever seen. Lord, have mercy, Jesus," She says, enroute to the kitchen for some fresh coffee, "Bobby B, do you want some coffee?"

"Yeah, I will take some. Remember, I like a lot of cream and sugar in mine." Bobby B pulls his cigar packet out of his pocket now. Billy Ray is watching him, and notices the packet in his hand. He knows that Hattie Mae doesn't normally allow people to smoke in her house. He starts whispering to his Uncle Bobby.

"Oooh, Uncle Bobby, are you getting ready to smoke? Grandma don't let folks smoke in her house...she gon' get you," Billy Ray is looking toward the kitchen.

"Lord, you are right. Uncle Bobby forgot! I told you I'm getting old," Bobby B says, and everybody in the room chuckles. He puts the cigar packet back in his pocket and starts reaching into the other pocket. "Let me see if I can find y'all some allowance money while I'm waiting on my fresh coffee."

Billy Ray starts jumping around as Bobby B is pulling out a stash of money. He takes six dollars out and passes each child two dollars. Hattie Mae walks in as he is giving the last two dollars. She hands him a cup of coffee, while he shoves the rest of the money into his pocket.

"Bobby B, you sho' got these kids spoiled. I don't know what we would do without you," Hattie Mae says, "These chitlins don't even let you breathe when you come around."

"We love our Uncle Bobby, Grandma! He is the best uncle in the whole wide world," Billy Ray says, still jumping around. He runs over and sits next to Bobby B, and the girls are quietly watching. Bobby B takes a sip of coffee and starts talking.

"I love y'all chitlins too, but I'm gon' have to get up and go in a little bit," He sets the coffee cup on the end table. A sad expression immediately flashes across Billy Ray's face; he is never ready for his Uncle Bobby to leave. One reason is because Hattie Mae always acts nice when Bobby B is around.

"Uncle Bobby, do you really have to leave right now?" Billy Ray pleads, "I want you to stay so we can play some Monopoly."

"Child, I hate to leave, but I promised my girlfriend I was going to take her somewhere. I know she's at the house, waiting on me," He says, pulling out his keys.

"Oh, yeah, that's right. I forgot, Grandma did say you have a woman," Billy Ray says, giving Bobby B some space. Bobby B shakes his head and laughs, and both girls are laughing, also.

Hattie Mae looks over at Billy Ray and starts talking, "Boy, what I tell you about flopping your mouth so much? Lord, have mercy, Jesus," She says, while everybody is still laughing.

Bobby B gets up and starts heading toward the door. He's almost at the door when he remembers he didn't kiss the kids goodbye.

"I forgot to get my goodbye kiss from y'all chitlins!"

The kids rush over to him, and he pecks them all on their cheeks. He starts turning the door knob, then turns to speak, "I'm gon' pick y'all up next weekend, and we're going fishing."

"Ooh, for real, Uncle Bobby? You really gon' take us fishing next Saturday?" Billy Ray says, before trying to jump as high as the ceiling, "Ooh, I'm so happy now! I might just see my Daddy on the fish bank!"

Bobby B doesn't respond, because he's clueless as to what Billy Ray is talking about. Once he makes it to his car, he suddenly recalls the story Hattie Mae told him about Billy Joe never returning home after a fishing trip. *Lord, I reckon that's what the poor baby is talking about...maybe he think he might run into Billy Joe on the fish bank...so sad, Lord.* He opens his car door and turns around, because he hears Billy Ray's voice.

Billy Ray is calling from the porch, "Uncle Bobby! Uncle Bobby! I'm gon' be waiting on you next Saturday!"

"Baby Boy, Uncle Bobby not gon' forget about y'all. Go on back in the house before you catch a cold. I see you don't have no shoes on," Bobby B says, while getting in the car.

"Ok. I love you, Uncle Bobby!"

"I love you, too, Baby!" Bobby B hollers, before cranking up his blue electric 225 vehicle. He backs out of the driveway, while Billy Ray heads back inside. Billy Ray starts jumping again, as soon as he is back in the house. Debra Anne is looking at him like he's crazy.

"Boy, why did you tell Uncle Bobby that you might see our Daddy on the fish bank? Don't you know you sound like a fool? You know Daddy died a long time ago," Debra Anne says, while staring at Billy Ray and shaking her head, "All I can say, is that you are just plumb crazy!"

Billy Ray rolls his eyes and then throws a paper ball at her. He stares for a few minutes before responding, "I'm not crazy, you stupid fool. Grandma said Daddy went fishing and he never came home. He still might be somewhere on that fish bank." Billy Ray looks disappointed despite his protests; in his little mind, he really wants to believe that his Daddy is still living. The girls know better, but he is too young to realize the unlikelihood of his desire.

"Billy Ray, don't you know that people don't live on the frickin' fish bank?" Debra Anne says, combing her long ponytail. She's looking at Billy Ray as if he has two heads. She waits a few minutes, then continues, "Boy, you say some of the stupidest things I've ever heard. I've just concluded that you don't have good sense!"

Hattie Mae and Lorretta Lynn had walked back to their rooms after Bobby B had left, and Hattie Mae overhears Debra Anne and Billy Ray in the living room, arguing. She decides to yell out from her bedroom,"What are y'all chitlins in there fussing about?"

"Billy Ray is in here calling me a stupid fool, Grandma. You already told him about calling people out of their names," Debra Anne says, while looking at Billy Ray and making a face.

Hattie Mae hollers back, while Debra Anne is shooting him a bird, "Boy, you betta stop calling your sister names, and get your butt somewhere and sit down. I bet' not hear you call her another name! Do you hear me, Boy?"

"Ok, slave master," He mumbles underneath his breath.

Hattie Mae couldn't hear him, of course, but Debra Anne could and did. She throws her comb down and runs back to Hattie Mae's room.

"Grandma! Grandma! Billy Ray just called you a slave master!"

Hattie Mae throws the bills down that she was sorting, and grabs her belt from the dresser. She jumps up and starts heading toward the living room, with a look from Hell on her face. Billy Ray notices her coming down the hall, and he jumps up and dashes out of the house with no shoes on. Hattie Mae is screaming while he's running out.

"I'm gon' tear your tail up! I'm gon' tear your tail up!"

Hattie Mae is ready to run out of the house with just a big housecoat on, and no bra. She gets as far as the porch, when Debra Anne shouts, "Grandma! Grandma! Don't step off the porch looking like that! What if the neighbors see you?"

Hattie Mae rushes back inside. By this time, the neighbors had spotted Billy Ray outside without shoes. Billy Ray is scared to death, and the look was painted all over his face. He's shaking like a leaf on a tree, and Ms. Penelope decides to scream across her yard.

"Hattie Mae! Hattie Mae! What on earth is wrong with your grandson out here? This boy don't have no shoes on and he look scared to death! What done happened up in that house?"

Hattie Mae doesn't dare let Ms. Penelope find out what's going on inside of her house. Everybody in the neighborhood thinks she's a saint and a good grandmother. She definitely doesn't want her image to be tarnished. She peeks her head out of the door and starts talking.

"How you? Child, ain't nothing wrong with that boy but that he's scared. He saw a big spider and ran out the house with no shoes on," She says, then hollers out to Billy Ray, "Child, get on back in this house before you catch a cold!"

Billy Ray is so glad that Ms. Penelope came outside and saved him. He starts easing his way back toward the house, looking around to make sure he doesn't step on anything.

Ms. Penelope starts talking again, "Well, I was just concerned, 'cause I noticed him in the yard with no shoes on. I know he's ok now, so I'm gon' go back in the house. It's a little chilly out here, I sho' don't want to catch no cold. Bye, Billy Ray!" Ms. Penelope waves and heads back to her front door.

Billy Ray doesn't say a word. He waves back and starts heading toward their house. He makes it to the front porch, and Hattie Mae is standing there, holding the door open. She doesn't have the heart to say anything or beat him now. She rolls her eyes and motions for him to go back to his room. Lorretta Lynn is in the living room, thinking about the lie her Grandma just told. Debra Anne had disappeared from the room after she started all the chaos, and the house is finally quiet again.

CHAPTER THREE

Two Days Later

"Grandma, I can I play in my room for a little while? I'm bored and it's too late to play outside," Billy Ray says, while Hattie Mae pulls her hair grease out from underneath the bathroom sink.

"Go on in your room and play. Don't you make too much racket, ok?" She replies, while walking to the kitchen with a straightening comb in her hand.

"What are you getting ready to do, Grandma? Are you getting ready to press your hair?" He asks, watching Hattie Mae turn on the kitchen stove.

"Yeah, I'm getting ready to run the comb through my hair. I've been putting it off all week. I hate tangling with this mess. Lord, my hair is getting gray," She says, looking in a mirror that was sitting on the kitchen table.

"Grandma, your hair is gray. Did my Momma have gray hair, too?"

"Naw, Baby. Your momma was young when she died. She didn't live long enough to get gray hair," She says, brushing the tangles out of her hair.

"Oh. You have to be old to get gray hair?" He looks sad.

"Yeah, usually you have to be old," She says, looking directly at Billy Ray, "Hey, I thought you wanted to go play in your room?"

"Yeah, I'm going pretty soon. Did my Mommy wear two braids like you do sometimes?"

Hattie Mae can sense that her grandson really misses his momma. She feels bad, because just the other day, he was focusing on his absent dad. Today, it's his momma. She sees pain all over his face, and decides to stop everything to talk to him.

"Baby, yo' Momma wore two braids down the middle of her hair when she was young. Although, she start wearing her hair down when she became a teenager. Sometimes, she would just put her hair up in a long pigtail. She had so much hair, whereas she really couldn't do a lot with it," She fights back tears as she reminisces about her deceased daughter. Her conversation was bringing back a lot of painful memories. She probably misses her daughter just as much as the kids do. She can tell that Billy Ray is feeling sad, so she holds back her tears. She decides to change the subject before she breaks down. "When are you going to play? It's gon' be time to go to bed soon," She says, putting the straightening comb on the stove.

"You are right, Grandma. It will be time for me to go to bed real soon. I guess I will go play now," Billy Ray says, skipping out of the kitchen.

The girls are sitting quietly in the living room. Lorretta Lynn is working on a crossword puzzle, and Debra Anne is writing in her journal, as usual. Billy Ray makes it back to his room and takes some trucks out. He starts playing, and the fishing trip crosses his mind. He puts his truck down and walks out to the bathroom, where Hattie Mae is still messing with her hair.

She looks up, startled to see his little head peeking in, "Boy, what are you doing?"

"Oh, I was just thinking about the fishing trip. Isn't Saturday the day that Uncle Bobby is coming to pick us up, Grandma?"

"Yes, Saturday is the day, but..."

"But what, Grandma?"

"I sure hope Bobby B don't end up disappointing you."

"Disappointing me? Why do you say that, Grandma?

"Child, you know how much your Uncle Bobby like to drink. Bobby B subject to get drunk and not even show up on Saturday," She says, walking out of the bathroom to put the straightening comb back on the stove. Billy Ray is following behind her like a little puppy.

"Grandma! Please don't say that. My Uncle Bobby has never told me a story."

She looks at Billy Ray while she is waiting on the comb to get hot. She can tell that he is anxious for a reply. She finally starts talking again. "I know he has never told you a story, but sometimes Bobby B get to drinking and he forget about things." She removes the pressing comb and starts heading back to the bathroom. Billy Ray follows behind her and pulls at her housecoat, trying to get her undivided attention.

Hattie Mae turns around, "Boy, what you pulling on my housecoat for?"

"I just want to let you know that I hope you are wrong. I'm gon' pray that my Uncle Bobby show up on Saturday," He says, while walking back to his room. He stops in his tracks. "Grandma...it smell like something is burning."

"It ain't nothing but a piece of hair done got on the stove."

"Oh. I was just wondering." He continues to his room, and decides to bend down beside his bed and pray.

Hattie Mae is almost done with her hair, and she's getting ready to go read her Bible. Both girls are watching T.V., and Billy Ray decides to go back to the living room and watch TV with his sisters. An old movie is on, and there's a very dark-skinned lady working as a maid for a wealthy family. Everybody is quiet until Debra Anne blurts out, "Lorretta Lynn!"

"Huh?" Lorretta Lynn says, shooting her sister a confused look. She's waiting patiently for Debra Anne to respond.

Debra Anne looks directly at her with a big smirk on her face, "Ooh, that black ugly maid that is on T.V. look just like your twin, Lorretta Lynn!" She bursts out laughing.

"What?!"

"You heard me!"

Lorretta Lynn is furious; she is having flashbacks about the night she had overheard Hattie Mae talking to Billy Ray. She looks at the TV again, and notices the lady scrubbing the floor. Debra Anne is still laughing, and Lorretta Lynn is fed up. She jumps up from the couch, grabs a big pillow, and throws it at Debra Anne as hard as she can. Debra Anne jumps and she's still laughing. Lorretta Lynn is so mad, she wants to knock her out. Instead of hitting her, she bursts into tears and runs to her room.

Billy Ray starts screaming at Debra Anne, "You're mean! You're mean! You are just like the wicked witch on the Wizard of Oz!" He says, as he rushes to the TV and changes the channels. He sticks his tongue out and runs to Hattie Mae's room.

"Boy, what are y'all doing in there? All y'all should be in the bed anyway! What on earth is wrong with you?"

"Grandma!" He says, while tears are forming.

"What, boy?"

"Debra Anne just made Big Sister cry. She told her she look like the black ugly maid on the TV show!" He explains, praying for some sympathy.

Hattie Mae shows no feelings; she just looks at him and starts talking, "Boy, don't you remember the night when we had the long conversation about your sister? Didn't I tell you that people who look like her work as maids and scrub rich white folks' floors?"

"Yes...yes, Grandma,"

"Well, what's your problem, then?"

"Well, my Uncle Bobby told me that nobody supposed to make fun of people because of their skin color or how they look," He says, while tiny tear drops are falling.

"Let me tell you one thing, boy, ain't nobody making fun of her. The truth is just the truth. You need to realize that you have a black ugly sister, and you betta thank God that you didn't come out looking like her. Go on to your room and go to bed. It done got real late."

Billy Ray decides not to say anything else. He's realizing that he's fighting a losing battle. He drops his head and walks out of Hattie Mae's room. The house is quiet, and his little mind is wandering. He prays silently, *God, my Grandma is so mean...I thought Grandmamas are supposed to love their Grandkids...how come my Mommy and Daddy had to die and leave us with her? Please help me and my big sister, God.* His little eyes tear up as he walks down the hall. He knows it's very late and he's supposed to be in bed. He doesn't care tonight. He just wants revenge. Billy Ray heads to the living room where Debra Anne is still up, watching TV, knowing nothing is going to happen to her. Hattie Mae always lets her get away with murder, and she takes advantage of that.

"What are you doing back in here? You betta go to bed before you get a beating," She says, with a smirk on her face.

"Shut up, you yellow banana! You don't tell me what do," He says, with anger painted all over his face.

"I rather be a yellow banana, than to be an ugly black monkey, like you-know-who," She says, sticking her tongue out.

Billy Ray had had enough tonight. His cup is overflowing and he can't take anymore. He rushes over to her so fast, she feels frightened. Before she has a chance to get up, he has hauled off and hit her. She tries to push him away, and he spits at her with full force. She's burning hot angry now; she reaches over and grabs his leg, then slams him down to the floor. She pushes him hard, and his head hits the metal train car that was laying on the floor.

Billy Ray's head starts bleeding, and he starts screaming at the top of his voice. Hattie Mae and Lorretta Lynn hear the commotion, and they rush to the living room. Lorretta Lynn sees him lying on the floor, and she hurries over to pick him up.

"What's wrong with y'all chitlins? Lord, what's wrong with y'all?!" Hattie Mae screams, "I ain't raise y'all like this," She shouts, walking to the hallway closet to get a towel for Billy Ray's head. "Lord, have mercy. Y'all chitlins gon' kill me one day!"

"Grandma, Billy Ray spit on me, and then I pushed him down. I didn't mean to hurt him, Grandma, I promise I didn't mean to hurt him," Debra Anne says, looking at the blood running from Billy Ray's head.

"Lorretta Lynn, wet this towel with some cold water and see if there's some peroxide in the bathroom medicine cabinet. Hurry up!" Hattie Mae says, "Billy Ray, you're gon' be ok."

Lorretta Lynn runs to the bathroom and wets the towel, then she pulls the peroxide out of the cabinet and runs back to the living room. She hands the towel and peroxide over to Hattie Mae. Hattie Mae places the cold towel on Billy Ray's head. He's talking now, so Hattie Mae looks over at Debra Anne.

"Y'all shoulda had y'all's tails in the bed, anyway. Lord, I'm getting so sick of y'all chitlins," She says, as guilt overcomes her spirit. She knows deep down inside that she's the culprit of all the commotion.

Lorretta Lynn looks over at her and starts talking, "Grandma, do you want me to find the Vaseline, too?"

"Yeah, I think it's sitting on my bedroom dresser."

"Grandma, am I gon' be alright?" Billy Ray asks, gently touching his head.

"Yeah, you gon' be fine. You just have a slight gash and bump on your head. It should be much better in a few days. Do you have a headache?" Hattie Mae asks, wiping a little blood off.

"No, I don't have a headache. My head is sore and it hurts a little. Am I still gon' be able to go fishing on Saturday, Grandma?"

"Yeah, you should be fine by Saturday," She says, while silently praying that Bobby B shows up, "You gon' have to sleep with me tonight, Boy".

"How come I have to sleep with you, Grandma?"

"Child, you bumped your head. I got to watch you for a while, just to make sure you are acting ok. I might have to call Bobby B, so he can take us to the hospital," she says, pecking him on the cheek.

"Grandma, what do you mean, if I am acting ok?"

"I just mean if you start acting confused, or if you head start swelling really bad," She says, and Lorretta Lynn is momentarily enjoying her Grandma's display of compassion.

"Ok, Grandma," Billy Ray says, while thinking, *maybe my Grandma really do love me and my big sister.* He drifts back when Hattie Mae starts talking.

"Come on, y'all, it's time for everybody to go to bed."

Debra Anne had left the room a long time ago. This is the first time she had actually felt guilty. Lorretta Lynn gives Billy Ray a big kiss, and says, "I love you, Baby Brother." She is silently thanking God for letting her baby brother be ok after his fall. She never wants to imagine life without Billy Ray. Everybody starts heading to their rooms. They are all tired, and it has been a really long day.

Two Days Later

Billy Ray is almost back to normal now. Hattie Mae is in the kitchen preparing breakfast, and the kids are getting ready for school. Hattie Mae puts a second batch of biscuits in the oven and walks back to the living room. She's watching the news, and she's interested in the news reporter's story about a rash of crimes in the area. She's thinking about how the small town is not as safe as it used to be. Her contemplation is disturbed by Billy Ray's voice.

"Grandma! Grandma!" He shouts from his bedroom.

"Yes, Boy?" She says, praying that he isn't getting ready to say that he felt sick from the fall.

"I smell something burning in the kitchen!"

"Oh, shit. Oh, shit! I forgot I left those biscuits in the stove," She says, rushing to the kitchen. She pulls the burnt biscuits out of the oven and places them on the counter. *Lord, I must be thinking about a black man.* She's remembering the old saying that goes, 'when you burn something up, you're thinking about a black man'. She refuses to throw the biscuits away, so she places them to the side, figuring she can give them to Lorretta Lynn.

The kids are still in their rooms, getting ready for school. Lorretta Lynn is looking for something cute to wear, and it's very challenging. Hattie Mae only purchases her clothes from the second-hand store. She finally stumbles upon some faded jeans with holes, and decides to dress them up with a nice top that Aunt Mamie had given her for Christmas. She is getting dressed when she hears Hattie Mae calling them to the breakfast table.

Lorretta Lynn starts rushing to put on her top, because the food smells so good. She buttons her jeans and puts on her loafer shoes. She's silently admiring the aroma of the food. It's been a long time since they had biscuits, sausage and grits; she opens up her bedroom door and starts walking to the kitchen.

"Ooh, Grandma. The food smell so good. I can't wait to eat!" Lorretta Lynn says, pulling a chair from the table.

"Did you wash your hands, Girl?"

"Yes, Grandma, remember? I just took a bath," She says, smiling at Hattie Mae.

Billy Ray and Debra Anne walk in, pull out their chairs and sit down. Hattie Mae is standing at the stove, preparing the plates. She takes the first batch of biscuits and fixes three plates. She reaches over and passes the first two plates to Debra Anne and Billy Ray. After that, she grabs two burnt biscuits and fixes a fourth plate. Lorretta Lynn is praying silently that Hattie Mae doesn't hand that plate to her. Hattie Mae had just showed compassion a few days ago; surely, she can't be back to her wicked ways this soon. Before she knows it, Hattie Mae is passing her the plate with the burnt biscuits.

Lorretta Lynn decides to speak up, "Grandma, why are you giving me the plate with the burnt biscuits?"

"It ain't gon' hurt you to eat those biscuits. You didn't think I was going to throw them away, did you?"

Disappointment flashes all over Lorretta Lynn's face. Billy Ray is watching, and he feels just as disappointed. How can his Grandma show compassion one day and switch right back to being mean a few days later? He drifts back from his thoughts as he hears his sister pleading for a good biscuit.

"Grandma, I don't want these burnt biscuits. Can I please have one of yours?" She says, with a pitiful look.

Billy Ray intervenes before Hattie Mae has a chance to answer, "You can have one of mine, Big Sister. I only need one," He says, passing his biscuit to Lorretta Lynn. As he was pulling his hand back, Hattie Mae hauls off and slaps it. Billy Ray is furious, and can't make sense of what just happened. "Grandma! Why did you just hit me?"

"Shut up, Boy, and eat your food!"

"You are so mean, Grandma! You are so mean!" He cries, before picking up his plate and slamming it to the floor. Glass splatters everywhere, and Lorretta Lynn is scared to death. Hattie Mae jumps up and starts walking over to the drawer where she keeps her belts. Billy Ray leaps to his feet and runs to his room. Lorretta Lynn is crying now, and she follows close behind him.

Hattie Mae has her belt and she's screaming toward the bedroom area, "Boy, you betta be glad you hurt yourself two days ago! If it wasn't for that, I would tear your tail up.

Y'all youngins grab y'all's school things and get out of here! I tell you the truth, y'all gon' kill me one day."

All three kids grab their bags and rush out of the front door.

CHAPTER FOUR

It's finally Saturday morning, and the kids are waiting around for Bobby B. Today is the day that they're going fishing, and Billy Ray can barely wait. He woke up early and he already has his fishing clothes on. He's pacing the floor when he's suddenly disturbed by the telephone ringing.

"Grandma! Grandma! Can I please answer the phone?" He calls out, while running toward the phone that was sitting on the living room table, "I know it's probably Uncle Bobby calling us."

"Go ahead and answer the phone, Boy." Hattie Mae is in the kitchen drinking coffee, and she's also praying that it's Bobby B. She's looking forward to getting a break from the kids today, because she often craves quiet time.

"Hello? Hello?" Billy Ray says, almost out of breath from running to the phone. It is Bobby B, and Billy Ray starts jumping when he hears his uncle's voice.

"Hi, Sugah. It's Uncle Bobby. Do y'all have your fishing clothes on yet?"

"Yes, Uncle Bobby, I have my fishing clothes on. I don't know about my sisters, though. Are you on your way right now?" Billy Ray asks, smiling from ear to ear.

"Yes, Sugah. I'm on my way right now."

"Ok, ok, I will tell my sisters," Billy Ray says, before slamming the phone down and jumping for joy. He runs to the back of the house, and screams toward the girls' bedrooms. "Big Sister and Debra Anne! Uncle Bobby just called and said he's on his way…yipee!" Billy Ray starts running to the hall closet in search of his fishing boots. He grabs his boots from the closet and dashes toward the couch. He dives onto the couch and starts putting his boots on. "Y'all better hurry up!" He shouts out to the girls.

"I know, I know! I already took my bath. I just have to put my fishing clothes on!" Lorretta Lynn hollers from her room.

Debra Anne doesn't say anything; she just continues to comb her long hair and put on her earrings. Debra Anne always likes to look prissy, regardless of where she is going. She's putting her hair in a ponytail, when she hears Billy Ray calling her name again. "What, Boy?" She snaps.

"Did you hear me say that Uncle Bobby is on his way?"

"Yes, Boy, I heard you," Debra Anne has an annoyed tone. *That boy act like he ain't use to going out the house...man, he is so worsome*, she thought to herself.

Hattie Mae is still in the kitchen, sipping on coffee and reading yesterday's paper. All of a sudden, she hears Billy Ray's rubber boots hit the kitchen floor. She looks up from the newspaper, and he's standing there, wearing a big smile.

"Grandma?"

"Yes, Boy? What do you want, smiling like a chess cat?"

"I told you I was going to pray that Uncle Bobby kept his promise. See, God answered my prayers, Grandma," He says, dancing around the kitchen.

"Sho' 'nuff. Well, just make sure you keep your fingers crossed, 'cause he ain't here yet," She says, worried that Bobby B may have stopped to get a drink on the way.

Billy Ray wasn't hearing it. He scratched his head and says, "Oh, he's coming, Grandma. God not gon' let Uncle Bobby disappoint me." He glances down at the rubber boots that Bobby B had bought for him. "How my new fishing boots look, Grandma?"

"Child, yo' boots look good. This is the first time you ever wore them, isn't it?"

"Yes, this is my first time. Remember, Uncle Bobby bought me these boots for my birthday?"

"Yes, Child, I remember," She says, getting up from the table and grabbing her broom, "Y'all ain't even had breakfast yet. Maybe I will just fix y'all some sandwiches for the road."

"You want me to help you clean up the kitchen, Grandma? I already have my fishing clothes on," Billy Ray says, waiting for Hattie Mae to respond.

"Naw, boy, and matter of fact, let me put this broom down. I need to be making y'all's sandwiches before Bobby B get here. You betta go back there and see what your sisters are doing," Hattie Mae says, opening the refrigerator.

"Yeah, you are right...let me go right now." Billy Ray starts skipping back to his sisters' room, and suddenly he hears a car pull up in the driveway. He backtracks and rushes over to the living room window to see if it is Bobby B. He notices the long, 225 car in the driveway, and starts jumping for joy. "Yipee! Yipee! It's Uncle Bobby in the driveway! Y'all betta come on!" He shouts at the top of his voice, and runs back into the kitchen.

"Grandma, do you think I might see my Daddy on the fish bank today?" He asks, with a dead serious look.

"Boy, yo' sister done told you that your Daddy is probably dead," Hattie Mae says, while wrapping peanut butter and jelly sandwiches.

"Yes, Grandma, I know she did say that, but remember? You said nobody ever found out the true story," Right then, he hears a knock on the door, and he forgets his conversation for a moment to answer it. "Uncle Bobby, I'm so glad you came! What was taking you so long outside?"

"Child, I was just out there straightening up my fishing stuff in the trunk."

"Did you catch some worms for us to take? I know sometimes you pick worms from your garden."

"Child, it ain't rained in a while, so we gon' have to buy some worms from the side of the road." Bobby B looks over at Hattie Mae while she's packing the lunches, "How are you doing, Big Sister? You are mighty quiet over there."

Hattie Mae is looking at her brother and smiling. "Brother, I am fine. I was just waiting on Billy Ray to stop talking. You know how he like to take up all your attention. It's hard to get a word in when he's around. How are you doing today?"

"Child, I'm fine, I'm fine. 'Bout good as an old man can be," He says, smiling and looking back at the girls' room.

"Brother, you ain't that old. They tell me you got so many women whereas you have to beat them off with a stick," Hattie Mae says, chuckling.

"Sho' 'nuff, Big Sister."

"Yes, Lord, that's what's singing in the streets, Baby Brother."

Bobby B chuckles and is getting ready to respond, when he hears all of the kids dashing down the hallway. Billy Ray had gone back to the girls' room and rushed them out.

"Uncle Bobby!" The girls say in unison.

"Yes, chitlins. Are y'all ready to go?"

"Yes, we are!" Billy Ray happily screams out.

"I'm ready for y'all to go, too," Hattie Mae says playfully.

"Big Sister, you know you gon' miss these chitlns. You ain't gon' know what to do with yourself today," Bobby B says, and notices Hattie Mae passing out the paper lunch bags, "I sho' hope you packed me a sandwich, too."

"Yes, I put you a salami and cheese sandwich in Billy Ray's bag. The kids all got peanut butter and jelly. I put some fruit and potato chips in the bags, too."

The kids grab their lunch bags, and Bobby B looks over at Hattie Mae, "Thank you, Big Sister, for packing me a lunch."

"Man, you ain't got to thank me. You know I'm gon' always look out for you. If it wasn't for you, me and these chitlins wouldn't be able to make it."

Bobby B chuckles, "That's what family is for," He turns to the kids and smiles, "Well, if y'all got all y'all's stuff, Uncle Bobby is ready to take a ride."

"Yes, Uncle Bobby, we are ready to go," Billy Ray says.

"Ok, let's get on out this house," Bobby B says, and everyone starts walking toward the front door. Billy Ray is the first out the door, as they say goodbye to Hattie Mae.

"Bobby B, drive careful! And y'all chitlins betta mind Bobby B, too," Hattie Mae says, while closing the living room door. She walks back to the kitchen and grabs the broom again. The house is quiet, and she's enjoying the peace. She sweeps the kitchen floor and then sets the broom down. She starts making a fresh pot of coffee, and sits at the kitchen table. She waits a few minutes for her coffee to brew, and then pours a mugful of the steaming liquid. Hattie Mae picks up her mug, heads to living room and grabs her Bible off of the end table. She reads for a while, and eventually falls asleep in her rocking chair.

Bobby B and the kids are driving down a dirt country road. Billy Ray is sitting in the back seat, and he has been staring out the window the entire time. All he's thinking about right now is spotting his Daddy. Bobby B slows the car down, because he notices a "Worms and Minnows For Sale" sign. He turns his car into a long, narrow driveway, and Billy Ray is wondering why they are stopping. He is so pre-occupied with finding his Daddy, he had forgotten they needed to stop for worms. He's been quiet during the drive and decides to break his silence. "Uncle Bobby, why are we stopping here? We're not at the fish bank."

"Oh, Billy Ray, remember, at the house I told you we have to stop for worms."

"Oh, that's right. I forgot already," Billy Ray says, paying close attention to his surroundings.

Bobby B makes it down the driveway and puts the car in park. They see a white man and a white woman seated on the front porch of the house. Bobby B gets out of his car, and the white man stands up to greet him.

"Howdy. You must be stopping here to buy some worms and minnows," The white man says, revealing that he doesn't have a tooth in his mouth.

"Yes'um. I was wondering if you have any left to sell?" Bobby B asks, glancing back at the kids, who are sitting patiently in the car.

"Yes'um, I still have some left, Mister. You got lucky, 'cause I'm almost out. How many dozens you need?" The old man heads toward the buckets where he keeps his worms and minnows.

"Oh, just give me two dozen of each. That oughtta do it for me," Bobby B says, with a cordial smile. Bobby B is very uncomfortable on this white man's property. He's trying his best to mask it, so he strikes up a conversation with the lady. "How are you doing today, Madam?"

"Oh, I do good, Mister. Just sitting here enjoying the nice, cool weather." She says, while her husband is walking back with a couple of cartons.

Bobby B notices the man returning, and he reaches into his pocket. "How much do I owe you, Sir?"

"Oh, just give me four dollars," the white man replies, while handing over the cartons.

Bobby B pays him, and is silently thanking God for protecting him and the kids. Bobby B knows he is in a prejudiced area, and he was taking a chance by stopping. Normally, he has his own worms, but he was running short because of the dry weather. He puts the worms and minnows in the trunk and climbs back into the car. He hadn't realized that the kids felt just as uneasy as he did. They weren't as familiar with racism, but something didn't feel right to them, either. He backs out of the driveway and starts heading toward the fish bank. Billy Ray goes back into a daze, observing every person and object that they pass. Not one time did he see anyone who resembled the father he never had a chance to know. Bobby B finally makes it to the fish bank. He pulls up, and he's looking for a parking spot. Billy Ray is anxiously waiting and observing all of the families. Bobby B finally parks and cuts the engine off. Billy Ray immediately jumps out the car and starts looking around at the men. All he can think about right now is finding his Dad. He looks around a little longer, then walks over to Lorretta Lynn and taps her on the arm. She's unpacking the fishing supplies

"Big Sister."

"Yes, Baby Boy?"

"Do you think my Daddy is out here with these people?" He says, looking so pitiful.

Lorretta Lynn hears the pain and sees the pain all over his little face. She feels bad and helpless at the same time. She reaches over and gives him a bear hug. "Baby Boy, I think your Daddy is in Heaven with Mommy and God."

"Yeah, but..." He trails off, with a sad look on his face.

Lorretta Lynn looks at him with compassion, "Give me a big kiss and we will talk later, ok?"

"Ok, Big Sister," He says, with puppy dog eyes.

Lorretta Lynn grabs her brother's hand and squeals, "Let's go catch Grandma some big fish! Come on, now, we got to catch up with Uncle Bobby and Debra Anne." She closes the trunk and grabs the fishing poles. The two start walking toward the river.

*****

Hattie Mae is piddling around the house, wondering what time the kids will be home. She figures they will catch some fish, so she decides to go in the kitchen and cut up some potatoes for French fries. After she finishes cutting up the potatoes, she mixes up some orange Kool-aid in a pitcher. She tries to call Mamie Lee again, but Mamie Lee's phone has been busy all day. Hattie Mae walks to her bedroom and grabs her yarn and needles. She sit down in her rocking chair in the living room, turns on the TV, and starts knitting. She knows the kids will be home soon, so she's trying to enjoy her last few moments of silence.

*****

It's dusk, and everyone is leaving the fish bank. Bobby B and the kids head to the car and start loading the trunk. Lorretta Lynn is excited, because she caught the biggest fish. Billy Ray is feeling down because he didn't see his dad. When the trunk is packed, they all jump in the car. Bobby B turns his head and looks at Lorretta Lynn and Billy Ray; he winks his eye and turns on the car. He backs out slowly, and Billy Ray is straining his little eyes. They get quiet, and each child falls asleep, one by one. Bobby B drives for miles, straining to keep his eyes open, too. He had stayed up the night before, courting his girlfriend, and he was feeling the effects of that now. He finally arrives at the house, and notices Hattie Mae has all of the lights on. *Maybe she missed the kids after all*, he muses. He turns the car off and starts waking up the kids.

"Debra Anne, Lorretta Lynn, Billy Ray,"

"Huh?" Billy Ray responds, while the girls are opening their eyes and yawning.

"Y'all can wake up now, 'cause we done made it home." Bobby B says, smiling.

"Aw, man, I can't believe I fell asleep," Billy Ray says, stretching and yawning.

"Boy, I can see why you fell asleep. You played hard with those other youngins. Let's get out this car and unload the fish. Y'all's Grandma got every light in the house on. She must be anxious for y'all to get in the house," He says, chuckling.

They roll out of the car and start unloading the fish. Hattie Mae is looking out the window now. Bobby B finally walks the kids up to the door and greets his sister. He knows Hattie Mae is going to cook the fish, but he can't stay for the fish fry. He had promised his girlfriend that he was going stop back over once he drops the kids off. He starts talking while the kids are running back to their rooms and the bathroom.

"Child, I'm gon' get ready to go. I enjoyed your youngins, but they're all yours, now," He chuckles, heading back to the front door.

"I sho' appreciate you giving me a break. You ain't gon' stay for some fish and French fries?"

"Naw, I promised my old lady that I was going to stop back by there," He says, smiling at his sister.

"Go on, Bobby B. Lord, I tell you the truth...you and your women," She says, returning his smile.

Billy Ray is back in the living room now, and he waves at Bobby B. He turns to Hattie Mae, "Grandma, we caught a lot of fish!"

"I'm glad. You see, I had all the lights on. I'm ready to get over to that stove and start frying y'all's fish. I sho' hate to clean them, though."

"I can't wait 'til you clean them and fry them! I'm getting right to my room and take off these dirty clothes," He says, skipping out of the kitchen. He stops and peeks his head into Lorretta Lynn's room.

She is startled for a moment, then laughs, "Boy, you scared me. I wasn't expecting to see your little head peeking in here."

"Grandma is getting reading to clean and cook our fish. She gon' make us some French fries, too! Ooh, I can't wait!" He skips away to his room.

Time passes, and the kids are spread out in the living room, playing Monopoly. Debra Anne is losing and getting upset, as usual. Billy Ray is getting hyper, because it's almost time to eat. The fish aroma is in the house, and he's sniffing his little nose. He starts talking while Lorretta Lynn is pulling a card.

"Man, I can't wait to eat some fish and French fries. It sho' smells good!" He says, smiling.

"Just hush up and play. I ain't never seen nobody who get so excited about some stupid food," Debra Anne says, while rolling her eyes.

"Oh, you're just mad because you are losing," He says, making a funny face.

"Shut up, Boy!"

"Y'all stop it! It's only a game!" Lorretta Lynn shouts.

They don't say anything back to Lorretta Lynn, and she's surprised. Debra Anne closes her eyes and mutters, "Please let me pick a good card..." She eases a card up, and opens her eyes. 'Go Straight To Jail' is the card that she picked.

Billy Ray jumps up, and says, "Go straight to jail, go straight to jail!"

Debra Anne throws her cards and money on the floor. Lorretta Lynn and Billy Ray are looking at her, and thinking the same thing: she is such a sore loser, they hate to play with her sometimes.

Lorretta Lynn starts talking as Debra Anne stands up. "Debra Anne, why do you always have to get mad when we are playing? It's only a Monopoly game."

"Shut up, you black heffa! I can act anyway I want to," Debra Anne says, rolling her hazel eyes.

Lorretta Lynn is in no mood to argue tonight. She just drops her head and starts collecting the pieces. Billy Ray is staring, because he still wants to play. He speaks up when she starts placing the pieces in the box.

"Big Sister, what are you doing? I still want to play," He says, with a puppy dog look.

"Naw,, we may as well stop playing. It's almost time to eat, anyway," She says, putting the top on the Monopoly game box.

"Let me ask Grandma if it is time to eat. Grandma!"

"Yes, Boy?"

"Is it time to eat yet?"

"Yes, the food will be ready in a few minutes. Go on in the back room and wash your hands," Hattie Mae hollers from the kitchen.

"Ok. I'm getting ready to go right now," He says, jumping up from the floor. He rushes down to the bathroom and grabs a tiny piece of soap. "Grandma, we don't hardly have any soap left!"

"Lord, have mercy," She hollers back, "you mean to tell me we done almost ran out of soap again? Y'all chitlins must eat soap. I reckon I'll have to borrow some from Ms. Penelope. Y'all just gon' have to use dish washing detergent 'til I walk over to Ms. Penelope's house."

"Ok...we still have a little piece left." Billy Ray washes his hands and runs out of the bathroom. He's running so fast he almost bumps into Debra Anne.

"Boy, you betta be glad you didn't hit me," She says, rolling her eyes.

"Shut up." Billy Ray snaps.

"Boy, who are you telling to shut up?" Hattie Mae asks, as soon as he walks into the kitchen.

"Oh, just Debra Anne. She's messing with me. I'm ready to eat now. Can I please sit at the table?"

"Go on, sit down, Boy."

"Grandma!" Debra Anne hollers from the bathroom.

"What, child? What do you want? You need to be in this kitchen. It's time to eat!" Hattie Mae is turning over a piece of fish in the skillet.

"I know, I'm coming. I just wanted to tell you that I found a bar of soap under the sink. It was way in the back! That's why Billy Ray didn't see it."

"Well, that's good. It should probably last us 'til I go to the market. I forgot I hid some soap back there."

Debra Anne opens the soap wrapper, and places the bar of soap on the sink. She brushes her long ponytail and flings it over her shoulder before walking out of the bathroom. When she sits at the kitchen table, Billy Ray starts talking to her.

"It sho' took you a long time in the bathroom. What were you doing in there?" He asks, eyeing the sizzling pans of food.

"Oh, I was just combing my long, pretty hair that your big sister don't have," She answers, slinging her ponytail again.

"Ahhh...you're just mad because my big sister beat you playing Monopoly."

"Where is your big sister?" Hattie Mae breaks into the conversation, "She should have already been in here." Hattie Mae is taking the second batch of French fries out of the skillet.

"Um...I don't know. She's probably in her room, reading." He turns and hollers over his shoulder, "Big Sister, Big Sister, what are you doing in there?"

"Oh, I'm coming. I'm just trying to sew the button back on my shirt." Lorretta Lynn answers from her room, where she is placing her shabby shirt back in her dresser drawer. She really doesn't have a lot of clothes, but she always tries to take good care of the few things she owns. She sets the needle and thread on top of her dresser and heads to the kitchen.

"Oh, Grandma, I forgot to tell you that I caught the biggest fish!" Lorretta Lynn smiles and waits for Hattie Mae's reaction. Hattie Mae ignores her and continues fixing the plates. She finally looks up Lorretta Lynn, and rolls her eyes. Lorretta Lynn just feels crushed. She drops her head and doesn't say another word. Billy Ray starts talking.

"Grandma, can I get the first plate?"

"Boy, why don't you stop acting like you never get anything to eat?" Hattie Mae snorts, while handing him his plate.

"I wish Uncle Bobby had stayed over and ate with us," He says, grabbing his plate.

"Boy, yo' Uncle Bobby had been with y'all all day. He had to go over yonder and see his girlfriend," She says, while setting the second plate on the table.

"What does 'over yonder' mean, Grandma? My teacher haven't taught me those words."

"Child, that's just a word that the old folks say. Eat your food and stop asking so many questions." She finally passes Lorretta Lynn her plate.

Lorretta Lynn is glad, and she looks over at Debra Anne. "Debra Anne, can you please pass me the hot sauce?"

Debra Anne shoves the hot sauce across the table, and it lands right on Lorretta Lynn's chest. Lorretta Lynn just shakes her head and Billy Ray rolls his eyes. Hattie Mae doesn't say a word; she sits down and starts eating.

"Ooh, this fish is good," Hattie Mae says, while smacking her lips. "Thanks, Debra Anne and Billy Ray, for catching Grandma some good catfish."

Lorretta Lynn feels left out, as usual. She drops her head and shovels in another mouthful of food.

"Grandma," Billy Ray says.

"What, Boy?"

"You forgot to thank Lorretta Lynn. Remember, she is the one that caught the biggest fish," He says, sipping his Kool-aid.

Hattie Mae is silent. Lorretta Lynn finishes her last bite of fish and stands up. *My Grandma always leaves me out, God. I guess she just hate me,* she thinks. She walks back to her room and closes the door.

CHAPTER FIVE

It's been a week since the fishing trip, and Hattie Mae is sitting at the table, reading her Bible. The kids are at school, and the house is as quiet as a cemetery. Hattie Mae gets up and starts fixing a fresh cup of coffee. The phone starts ringing just as she's pouring her coffee. Hattie Mae sets her coffee down, and walks over to the phone that is sitting on the kitchen counter. She picks it up and starts talking.

"Russell's residence."

Mamie Lee is on the other end of the phone. "Hi, Big Sister, how are you doing?"

"Lord, have mercy. Mamie Lee, I ain't heard from you in ages. I was wondering if you forgot I was still living," Hattie Mae says, chuckling, "how are you doing?"

"I'm doing good, and yes, it has been a long time. What are you doing right now? Buck and I are thinking about coming over."

"Child, I ain't doing nothing but sitting on my rump, drinking some coffee. Y'all come on over here. I'll be waiting, ok?"

"Ok. We will see you in a little while. Please make me a fresh pot of coffee, Big Sister."

"Ok, I will. Y'all drive safe, and I will see y'all soon."

"Ok." Mamie Lee says, before hanging up the phone. She's looking forward to seeing Hattie Mae. She hasn't been over to her house since the dinner incident with Lorretta Lynn. She doesn't like how Hattie Mae treats Lorretta Lynn, but she still can't help but love her sister. Her mother had always taught her to love her siblings, no matter what.

Hattie Mae is moving around, trying to straighten up the living room. Toys are scattered everywhere, and plant dirt is all over the floor. She picks up the toys and throws them in the toy box. She then pulls the fragile old broom with most of its straw missing out of the closet. She sweeps the floor, then walks over to the kitchen cabinet and pulls out the coffee grounds. She pours the coffee mix in the pot, then adds the water. She places the pot on the stove and walks back to her bedroom. She is standing in her room, in a daze. She's trying to figure out which outfit to put on; she doesn't have a lot of clothes, because most of her money goes toward taking care of the kids. Hattie Mae decides to slip on her floral printed housedress.

Hattie Mae walks to the bathroom and grabs her hair grease from underneath the sink. She then pulls her comb out, and parts her silver hair down the middle. She braids her hair into two braids, one on each side, and returns the comb to the drawer. She starts brushing her teeth, but she's disturbed by a knock on the door. *Lord, that must be Mamie Lee and Buck. They sho' got over here fast!* She rushes out of the bathroom, full of joy.

"Who's knockin'?"

"Child, it's me and Buck. Open up this door."

Hattie Mae is smiling from ear to ear while she unlocks the door. "Lord, have mercy, come on in, child. I'm so glad to see y'all!" She stretches out her arms to hug Mamie Lee and Buck.

"Child, we are glad to see you, too. You got my hot coffee ready?" Mamie Lee says, while she and Buck are removing their coats.

Hattie Mae is listening to Mamie Lee, but staring Buck up and down. Buck is wearing an outfit that only a clown should wear. His pants are hi-water, and his shirt has bright checkers stamped all over. His suspenders are brown, and he's wearing a wide-brimmed, caramel colored hat. His hat is cocked to the side, and Buck really thinks he is sharp. Hattie Mae is stunned by Buck's outfit and she can't hold her peace anymore. She looks at Mamie Lee, and then back to Buck. She starts talking while she's attempting to hang up their coats.

"Buck?"

"Yes, Big Sister?"

"I just have one question for you. Where on earth did you get that outfit from?" She says, wide-eyed and as serious as a heart attack.

As usual, Buck doesn't reply. He just chuckles and looks over at his wife, who has always rescued him. Mamie Lee doesn't appreciate Hattie Mae's comments, and she decides to speak up.

"I thought you supposed to be in the kitchen fixing us some coffee, and here you are in here, worrying about my husband's outfit," Mamie Lee says, staring Hattie Mae down.

"Child, that coffee ain't going nowhere. I'm just trying to figure out how you let Buck come out the house looking like this?"

"Looking like what, Hattie Mae?"

"Did you say, looking like what? Mamie Lee, have you gone blind?"

"Child, he look fine to me and he's clean," She says, checking her husband out, "I know my husband might not be the best dresser, but he's a good man and he's a hard-working man." She looks back at her big sister.

"Child, I don't care if he is a good man. I wouldn't be seen at the mess house, wiping my tail, with a man looking like Buck."

Hattie Mae has struck a nerve. Mamie Lee was sitting down, but she suddenly jumps up. She puts her hand on her hip and cocks her head to the side. Hattie Mae is wondering what she is getting ready to say.

"Big Sister, I am getting ready to give you a piece of my mind. How dare you talk about my good man?" She says, waiting on Hattie Mae to challenge her.

"Child, what does a good man have to do with looking like a clown?" Hattie Mae chuckles.

"Well, he might not be the best dresser in town, but he's way better than that old joker you had for a husband." Mamie Lee follows Hattie Mae to the kitchen. Hattie Mae chuckles again, while removing the coffee from the stove. She tries to change the subject, but Mamie Lee won't let her. "Child, I ain't finished with you yet. Don't be trying to change the subject."

"Mamie Lee, you ain't gon' let this conversation go, are you?"

"No, Ma'am. You talked about my husband, so I am getting ready to talk about that old joker you had. That old Negro couldn't even hold a job at Pat & Turner," She says, pulling a chair from the table.

"Pat & Turner? Who in the world is Pat & Turner, Mamie Lee?" Hattie Mae says, with a confused look.

Mamie Lee pauses for dramatic effect. She looks straight at Hattie Mae and says, "Patting up and down the streets and turning corners all damn day!"

Hattie Mae grabs a magazine and playfully acts like she is getting ready to hit her sister. The two start to chuckle, and then they're disturbed by a knock on the door.

"Lord, who is knocking at my door? Ain't nobody else called and said they were coming over," Hattie Mae says, heading to the front door.

"Child, it might be Bobby B. I sho' hope so, cause I ain't seen him in a while."

Bam! Bam! Bam! The knocks are loud and persistent. "Lord, it must be Bobby B, 'cause he's the only person that knock that hard," Hattie Mae says, then calls out, "who is it?"

It was Bobby B, and his voice is slurred. He is so intoxicated, he can barely say his name straight. Hattie Mae opens the door when she realizes that it is him. The strong smell of alcohol nearly takes her breath away. She opens the screen door, while Bobby B staggers in. Hattie Mae is disgusted, and starts talking.

"Lord, have mercy. Come on in, Baby Brother, before you fall on the porch and my neighbors see you. Lord, have mercy. You are drunk as a skunk."

Bobby B is just staring at her with glazed eyes. He's sharp as a tack, as usual. He's wearing a camel colored leisure suit, and a camel colored wide-brimmed hat. His pointed brown shoes are so shiny, they literally could blind someone. Hattie Mae is so upset that he's drunk, but Mamie Lee really doesn't care. Mamie Lee is just happy to see her brother.

Hattie Mae straightens her big house coat and starts talking, "Bobby B, what on earth are you doing, drunk in the middle of the week? Lord, have mercy, Jesus. You usually wait at least until the weekend. Take a seat and let me fix you some coffee," Hattie Mae makes her way back to the kitchen.

Mamie Lee walks into the living room, "Baby Brother, I'm so glad to see you. How have you been?" She asks, even though she knows he can't answer her right because he's drunk.

"I ain't...I ain't...doing...doing too good, Mamie Lee. My old lady, Lula...Lula...Lula Bee fired me today," He says, while trying to keep a straight face.

Hattie May overhears some of his conversation from the kitchen. When she hears the word 'fired', she immediately puts the coffee down and rushes to the living room. She is walking so fast, she almost loses her balance. She looks at Bobby B with a pitiful look. "Bobby B, you mean to tell me that you done got fired from that good railroad job? What in the world did you do to make that white man fire you? Lord, have mercy, Jesus. What are me and these kids going to do now?" She says, shaking her head.

Mamie Lee is waiting on Hattie Mae to stop talking. *Lord, my sister sho' need to wear her hearing aid,* she's thinking. Hattie Mae is so disgusted, she just turns around and starts heading back to the kitchen. Mamie Lee calls her name while she is walking.

"Hattie Mae!"

"I hear you, Child. Lord, I'm so disgusted, that I don't know what to do,"

"Big Sister, you didn't even hear Baby Brother right,"

"What you talking about, Mamie Lee?"

"I'm talking about the fact that he didn't say nothing about the railroad firing him. I done told you over and over that you need to wear your hearing aid."

"Sho' 'nuff? I thought that's what he said," Hattie Mae says, wearing a smile of relief now, "Well, what did he say, then?"

"He said his good thang, Lula Bee, fired him today."

"Lord, I guess I do need to wear my hearing aid," Hattie Mae says, chuckling with relief.

Buck seldom talks, but he decides to say something now. He looks over at Bobby B, "Bobby B, you mean to tell me you lost your good thang, Lula Bee? Lord, I ain't had no good thang in a long time," He mumbles.

Mamie Lee heard Buck's mumbling, and she jumps up from the couch. "Man, what did you just say? Let me go in the kitchen and get that black skillet!" She rushes toward the kitchen.

Buck's eyes bulge, and he jumps up and runs toward the back of the house. Mamie Lee has the skillet now, and she starts running behind him. Then she realizes what she is doing, and stops in her tracks. She hollers out to Buck, "You betta stay yo' rump in that room, before I knock some sense in yo' head!"

Mamie Lee heads back to the kitchen table and picks up her mug of coffee. Hattie Mae and Bobby B had ignored all the commotion. Bobby B staggers over to the family record player that he had purchased, and cranks up the music. He turns the music up so loud, both sisters plug their ears. Buck hears the loud music and comes back to the living room. He takes a seat on the couch and acts like nothing ever happened. After a while, the two men get up and start dancing around the living room. The sisters are in the kitchen, drinking coffee and catching up on church and neighborhood gossip.

Chapter Six

Next Month

Debra Anne and her two light-skinned friends, Sheila and Kelly, are standing outside, waiting on the school bus. They spot Lorretta Lynn with her friends in another area, and Sheila turns to Debra Anne.

"Debra Anne?"

"What, girl?"

"Is that your black ugly sister standing over with those ugly girls?"

"Yep. That's her ugly black butt. My Grandma always say she is a disgrace to our family."

"Which one is she?" Kelly asks.

"The one who is wearing the short pigtail, and looks like a monkey." Debra Anne says, while pointing at Lorretta Lynn.

"Oh, for real? That's your sister?" Kelly says in disbelief, "Man, she don't look nothing like you. How can you be so light and pretty, and she is so black and ugly?"

"Well, she have a different daddy than me and my baby brother. Grandma say her daddy and his whole family were black and ugly."

"Well, all of her friends' family members must be black and ugly, too. They look like three little peas in a pod," Kelly says, before they all burst into laughter.

Lorretta Lynn sees her sister and the other girls laughing. She's trying to figure out what's so funny. Tobbey notices her looking over at Debra Anne.

"Who are you looking at over there, Lorretta Lynn?" Tobbey says, with a curious look on her face.

"Oh, I'm just looking at my sister and her friends. I'm trying to figure out why they're laughing so hard."

"They sure are laughing a lot. They must be having a good time talking about something. I wonder what's so funny?" Tobbey says, staring at the girls.

"I don't know, but I'm getting ready to ask her," Lorretta Lynn says, cupping her hands around her mouth.

"You gon' have to scream real loud. They are way over there," Tobbey says.

"I know, but I have a big mouth. Watch me," Lorretta Lynn says. They all giggle, and she hollers, "Debra Anne...Debra Anne...what y'all laughing at?"

Debra Anne ignores her and continues laughing with her friends. Lorretta Lynn and her friends are waiting patiently; they figure maybe they can get in on a good laugh. They would have never thought Debra Anne and her friends were laughing at their dark skin color. Lorretta Lynn decides to scream her question again.

"Debra Anne, did you hear me? We want to know what's so funny!"

All of the girls can tell that Debra Anne's getting ready to respond now. Debra Anne screams at the top of her voice:

"We're laughing at you, little black monkey!"

"Wait a minute. Did she say what I think she just said?" Tobbey says, with anger all over her face.

"Yes, she did, Tobbey. Let's go kick her butt!" Jollie says, and they both take off running. The girls were running so fast, anyone would have thought they were in a relay match. Lorretta Lynn is scared now, and she starts crying and trembling. As bad as Debra Anne treats her, Lorretta Lynn still doesn't want anyone to hurt her sister. She wants to run, but she's too nervous. She starts screaming at the top of her voice:

"Tobbey! Jollie! COME BACK! COME BACK! Please don't bother my sister! Oh, please don't hurt her!" She is getting hysterical, screaming and shaking, and her friends finally listen to her plea. Both girls are almost out of breath, as they turn around and start walking back toward Lorretta Lynn. Debra Anne and her friends had jumped on the bus, and they were gone. Lorretta Lynn is wiping her tears, as the girls make it back to her side. The girls get on the bus, and the Caucasian bus driver doesn't say a word. He just closes the bus door and starts driving away.

When Lorretta Lynn makes it home from school, she walks in the house and notices that it is empty. She sees a note on the kitchen table, and reads,

We are gone to the market. I cooked some pinto beans and cornbread. We shouldn't be gone too long.

Lorretta Lynn sets the note down and starts reflecting back to her long day at school. "Lord, will my life ever get any better? I just don't know how much longer I can live this nightmare," She prays out loud, "maybe I will feel better after I eat my pinto beans and cornbread. After all, it is one of my favorite meals, God."

Lorretta Lynn puts her book bag down, and walks back to the bathroom to wash her hands. Then, she heads to her room to change. Feeling somewhat refreshed, she walks to the kitchen to fix her plate. She pours a big glass of grape Kool-aid, and sets it by her food. She can't wait to drink it, because it's been such a long, hard day. She's thinking about how things would have been different if her mom hadn't died, and she silently thanks God for giving her Billy Ray. She eats her beans and cornbread and gets up from the table to pull out her homework. Suddenly, she is disturbed by a knock on the door. She can't imagine who it can be; she puts her homework down and walks to the front door.

"Who is it? Who is it?" She says, in a low voice.

"Oh, it just Mr. Fred, sweetie. I'm yo' Grandma's friend. You know, the man that always give y'all free fruit and vegetables. I have some fresh fruit that I need to drop off."

"Oh, ok."

"Is yo' Grandma home?" He asks, while Lorretta Lynn is unlocking the door. She ignores him, because for some reason, she's feeling uneasy. She notices his drunken face, and wonders if she should completely open the door. Then she thinks about how they can always use some free food. She pushes away her thoughts, and completely opens the door.

"Hi, Sugah. How are you doing today?"

"Oh, I'm ok. I'm ok," She says, trying not to gasp at the strong alcohol smell emanating from the man's body.

"Is yo' Grandma home? She normally answer the door when I stop by."

"Oh, um, my Grandma went to the market. She should be home in a few minutes," She says, and her voice is trembling. She doesn't like being alone with a drunk man.

"Sho' 'nuff. Where's your sister and brother?" He says, still holding the fruit basket, "I know Hattie Mae ain't left you home by yourself."

"Um, yeah, but she should be home soon. You can just leave the fruit basket on table, Mr. Fred," She says, as an uneasy feeling is creeping over her body.

Mr. Fred starts looking her up and down. She has always felt uncomfortable around him, but this is the first time that she has ever been alone with him. Something just doesn't feel right, and she's praying silently that he hurries up and leaves. She reaches for the fruit basket, and he ignores her. He starts walking toward the kitchen, and she follows hesitantly.

"Mr. Fred, you don't...have to go in the kitchen...I can put the basket up," She says, but he keeps walking.

"Oh, I can sit it on the table, Sugah," He's looking at her like she's a piece of meat.

"Oh...ok...ok...I'll wait so I can lock the door after you leave," She says, nervously twisting her small ponytail.

He plops the basket down, then whirls around and starts walking toward Lorretta Lynn. She's praying for him to leave, but her intuition is telling her something different. *Maybe I should just pick up the phone and call my Uncle Bobby*, she thinks. He's really staring now, and he's moving closer and closer. She's trying to walk him to the front door, and he quickly grabs her.

"Mr. Fred! Mr. Fred, why are you putting your hands on me?" She cries, shaking like a leaf. She tries to pull away from him, but he grips her tighter. She yanks away and starts running to the back of the house. She tries to pick up the phone that was sitting on the hallway table, but he forcefully snatches it from her. She starts running again, and he rushes up and grabs her from behind.

"Leave me alone! Leave me alone!" Lorretta Lynn yells, but he pushes her into her bedroom and throws her onto the bed. "Get away from me! Get away from me, you dirty old man!" She starts screaming at the top of her voice, and he slams his smelly hand over her mouth.

"Don't you move! Don't you move! I will take my knife out and cut your throat. I been looking at you for a long time. I knew one day I was gon' catch you alone," He snarls, while fumbling with his zipper. Lorretta Lynn tries to get up from the bed, but he shoves her back down and starts pulling up her play skirt. She starts screaming again, and he digs in his pocket for a hand knife. He flicks open his knife and points it at her throat.

"You betta lay on this bed while I pull your panties off. If you say one mo' thing, I'm gon' cut your throat."

Lorretta Lynn is tired of fighting, and she surely doesn't want to die. He finally puts the knife down and forcefully pries open her legs. He drops his pants and enters into her small-framed body. He starts raping her brutally, as she cries and struggles. She manages to push her hand between their private areas, and pulls it back when she feels something wet. He sees blood on her hand, and jumps back. He pulls his pants up and rushes out of the bedroom, trying to straighten his clothes. He stumbles through the living room and out the front door.

Lorretta Lynn hears the echo of the front door slamming, as she's lying on her bed in shock. *Oh God, why me? Oh, why me? Maybe I am a black curse, God.* She rolls off the bed, and grabs at her sweat pants, which were draped on the side of her bed. She's shaking as she reaches for a pair of clean panties. It's hard to pull them up with trembling limbs and the pain that is wracking her whole body, but she's determined to look normal before Billy Ray gets home. After she slowly manages to get dressed, she sees her mother's Bible on her nightstand, and picks it up. Lorretta Lynn curls up on her bed and starts praying as she cracks open the Bible.

Hattie Mae, Billy Ray and Debra Anne arrive home a few minutes later. Billy Ray starts sniffing as soon as he walks in. Hattie Mae notices his facial expression, and comments, "Boy, why are you sniffing your nose?"

"Something smells like...alcohol in this house," He says, dropping the grocery bag on the couch.

"Boy, I don't smell no alcohol. That's all in your mind," She says, walking to the kitchen with grocery bags in her hands. Billy Ray ignores her comment and runs down the hall in search of Lorretta Lynn. He peeks his head inside, and sees her sleeping. Lorretta Lynn isn't asleep, but she feels it's best to pretend. He closes the door gently and skips back to the living room. She continues to lay there, silently talking to God about her horrible day.

Hattie Mae and the other kids are in the kitchen now. Billy Ray and Debra Anne are putting away groceries, while Hattie Mae begins to make an apple pie. Billy Ray opens the kitchen drawer and puts the Kool-aid away. He shuts the drawer and looks over at Hattie Mae, "Grandma?"

"Yes, boy. "

"How come Ms. Penelope's car is so loud? It sound just like an old truck. I'm glad my friends didn't see us coming from the market," He says, looking at Hattie Mae with an embarrassed expression.

"Boy, what'd I tell you about talking about folks? You oughtta be glad we got a neighbor to run us to the market sometimes. Everybody don't have no money to buy a nice car like your Uncle Bobby and Aunt Mamie Lee," She says, pouring some flour out of the canister.

"I know, Grandma, but it's just embarrassing to ride in a raggedy car."

"Yeah, I know, but a lot of colored folks in this small town don't have no money. They are lucky just to be able to put food on their table."

He looks at Hattie Mae for a second, then peeks his head into another grocery bag. "You bought some good food today, Grandma. We got potato chips, ice cream, graham crackers and ginger snaps. It's been a long time since you bought this much food. Uncle Bobby must have gave you some money."

Hattie Mae looks at him and chuckles. "Yeah, your Uncle Bobby worked some overtime, so therefore he was able to give me a piece of change. He made me promise that I would buy y'all a lot of junk food. I decided I betta do what he told me to do," She says, smiling and silently counting her blessings.

"Well, thanks, Grandma. Looks like we gon' eat good for a long time. Mr. Fred must have dropped the fruits and vegetables off when we were at the market. Did you see them sitting over there on the counter?"

"Yes, I sho' did."

His eyes are wide, as he dances around, looking at all of the good food. He's feeling happy and decides to ask if he can turn on the record player. Hattie Mae nods her head and starts talking while he is fiddling with the record player.

"What is your big sister back there doing? Normally, she would have been in here by now."

"Big Sister was asleep when I went to her room. I guess she must be really tired today. I'm gon' cut the record player on now, ok?" He says, opening the top of the record player.

"Boy, you love music just like yo' Momma did. I believe that's why she got tied up with your big sister's Daddy, 'cause he played in a band," Hattie Mae shouts from the kitchen.

It isn't long before the apple pie is smelling good, and Hattie Mae is just as excited to bite into it as the kids. She pulls the ice cream out of the freezer and removes four small bowls from the cabinet. She calls Billy Ray's name, "Go back there and wake your big sister up. Her lazy butt been in the bed since we got home from the market. I'm surprised that loud music hasn't woke her black tail up."

Billy Ray stops dancing and runs back to Lorretta Lynn's room. He opens the door and notices that she is still lying in bed. Her eyes are open now, and he's glad.

"Big Sister, Big Sister, get up. Grandma made us a homemade apple pie. She said you need to come to the kitchen so we can eat some apple pie and ice cream!" He rattles the words off, before rushing back to the living room to enjoy the music.

Lorretta Lynn slightly smiles, and motions an acknowledgment. Normally she would be excited, but not today. She's in a lot of pain, and really doesn't have the strength to get up. She struggles to shift her body off of the bed, because she knows what the consequences will be if she disobeys. She definitely can't stand a beating today. She grabs her house coat from the dresser and wraps it around her aching body. She's moving at a snail's pace, and Hattie Mae is calling her name.

"I'm coming, Grandma, I'm coming," Lorretta Lynn says in a weak tone, "it's taking me long because I'm not feeling good." She slowly creeps to the living room. *Oh God, please help me,* she's thinking. She finally makes it to the kitchen, and Billy Ray can tell something is wrong. He looks up from dessert and starts talking.

"What's wrong with you, Big Sister? You look so sick," His concern shows on his face.

"Ohh...I'm just not feeling good, Baby Brother. I'm gon' be ok, though," She says, noticing Hattie Mae's mean look, "is the apple pie good?" She tries to change the subject.

"Uh huh, it's good. Why do you look like you're in so much pain?"

She is in excruciating pain and can't hold it in any longer. She decides to speak up and at least tell a little bit about what happened while they were at the market. *Maybe I'll just say Mr. Fred was reeking with alcohol, and it literally made me sick to my stomach.* She hesitates, and then starts talking, "Grandma, Mr. Fred dropped off a fruit basket while you were at the market and..."

Hattie Mae belligerently interrupts her. "Don't you know I see that fruit basket sitting over there, stupid girl? Hush yo' mouth and start eating!" She glares at Lorretta Lynn.

Loretta Lynn falls silent, and her siblings don't say a word. This is the first time that Debra Anne actually feels bad for Lorretta Lynn. She's thinking about what happened at school today, and her conscience is tearing her up. If silence could kill, the whole room would be dead by now.

CHAPTER SEVEN

The next day, Hattie Mae wakes up and looks at the clock on her nightstand. *Lord, I almost over slept today!* She never sets the alarm, because she usually wakes up on time. She jumps up, because she doesn't want the kids to be late for school. She leaves her room and heads toward the kids' rooms.

"Billy Ray, Debra Anne, Lorretta Lynn! Y'all get y'all's tails up. It's time to get ready for school. Y'all better hurry up, cause I already done overslept."

All of the kids except Lorretta Lynn respond. She peeks in Lorretta Lynn's room, and notices she is still lying in bed. Hattie Mae can tell Lorretta Lynn has no intention of getting up. She's angry now, and she starts screaming so loud that her voice echoes throughout the entire house.

"Didn't I tell you to get your tail out of the bed? I know you heard me say that I had already overslept! Get your black tail up right now!" Hattie Mae is screaming, but Lorretta Lynn is not moving. Hattie Mae is furious, and she rushes over to Loretta Lynn's bed, shouting, "Do I need to get my belt out and speed yo' monkey-looking tail up?"

"Grandma! Grandma! Please don't get your belt out and beat me! I'm still in bed 'cause I'm still not feeling good!" Lorretta Lynn pleads, before bursting into tears.

Hattie Mae ignores her. "I'm going to get my damn belt now!" She is shouting and slamming the bedroom door. Billy Ray had overheard the whole conversation, and he ran into the living room to hide both of her belts. Hattie Mae notices him coming back down the hall, looking scared. She pushes him aside, "Get out my way, Boy. I got to find my belt. I'm getting ready to tear her black tail up!"

Billy Ray doesn't say anything. He just tiptoes to the kitchen and finishes eating his cereal. Debra Anne is eating also, and Hattie Mae is searching for her belt.

"I can't find my belts! Lord, have mercy. Y'all chitlins are always moving my stuff."

Billy Ray decides to try distracting her. "Grandma, can we have our lunch money? You betta hurry up, cause we might end up missing the bus."

Hattie Mae stops searching for a moment, and heads over to her bag, which is sitting on an end table. She picks it up and digs inside for her change purse. Hattie Mae gives the two kids their lunch money and they rush out the door. Billy Ray is praying silently that Hattie Mae doesn't beat his sister once he leaves. Hattie Mae's pale face is red, and she forgets about finding her belt. Mamie Lee's voice is ringing in her head: "You are going to hell. You are going to hell. You betta stop mistreating that child." She takes a deep breath, and heads to the kitchen to start making fresh coffee.

Lorretta Lynn is still lying in bed. The sound of the door slamming is ringing in her ears. Tears are still pouring from her eyes. All she's trying to figure out is why God even allowed her to be born. No child should have to go through what she's going through. On one hand, she wants to tell Hattie Mae what Mr. Fred had done, and on the other hand she feels that Hattie Mae won't care anyway. She grabs her mother's Bible and starts reading; after she reads a few passages, she decides to pick up her school book. *Maybe if I study, it will ease my mind, God.* She starts reading her lessons, trying to forget about the horrible two days.

Hattie Mae is still in the kitchen, and she's thinking about her granddaughter. She really believes nothing is wrong with Lorretta Lynn. The more she thinks about her lying in the bed, the angrier she becomes. She decides to walk back to the child's room and open the door. Lorretta Lynn is still studying and Hattie Mae just stares at her with a look from Hell. Lorretta Lynn notices her staring.

"Hi, Grandma. Do you need me for anything?" She says, in a soft voice. Hattie Mae is glaring, and Lorretta Lynn is wondering what is coming next. She braces herself, because she knows it's nothing good.

Hattie Mae breaks into her thoughts with a hideous tone of voice: "I know you are just playing hooky, and I just want to let you know one thing: you bet' not get out that bed for one damn thing! I shouldn't even let you go to the bathroom. I should let you piss in your clothes and just lay in 'em!" She says, then slams Loretta Lynn's door.

"Grandma. Grandma!" Lorretta Lynn screams out. Hattie Mae ignores her, and starts walking toward the kitchen. Lorretta Lynn is fed up. She just can't take it anymore. Her heart is racing, as she slowly eases up from the bed. She grabs her housecoat and gingerly puts it on. She takes a look in the dresser mirror, and thinks she looks exactly how she feels. She brushes those thoughts away, and opens up her bedroom door. She needs to confront Hattie Mae, and it's happening now. She creeps to the kitchen and notices Hattie Mae sipping on coffee and reading her Bible. Loretta Lynn decides to let her have it.

"Grandma! Grandma!" She screams, and Hattie Mae looks at her like she has grown two heads.

"Child, what on earth is wrong with you? How dare you, coming in my kitchen, screaming out my name like a maniac! Don't you know, I will slap the piss out of you, Girl!"

Lorretta Lynn is standing tall, and this is one time she is not afraid. She's staring at Hattie Mae, and she's searching for the right words to say. Her fury rises when she notices Hattie Mae holding the Bible. She looks directly into Hattie Mae's eyes, and starts speaking in a low, serious tone.

"Look at you. Sitting over there, acting like you are a Christian, holding God's Bible in your hand. You oughtta be ashamed of yourself, Grandma. You ain't nothing but a devil walking around in sheep's clothing. All my life, you've done nothing but mistreated me. I hope you know, God is watching you, and if you make it to the pearly gates, you're gonna pay! Now, go ahead and make my day. Slap the piss out of me!" She says, while tears are welling in Hattie Mae's eyes. Lorretta Lynn is still standing, and she's thanking God silently for the strength to do something that was way overdue. Lorretta Lynn gently turns around and starts tip toeing back to her room.

Hattie Mae is shocked. She has never seen this side of Lorretta Lynn. She continues to cry, and stares down at her

Bible. This is the second time she had heard that "God is watching you." She starts praying, begging God for forgiveness.

It's almost time for the kids to get out of school. Lorretta Lynn is still in her room, and she has only come out to use the bathroom. Hattie Mae is sitting in her rocking chair, and she's grasping hard to her Bible. Her fight with Lorretta Lynn has been heavy on her mind. This is the first time in her life that she's actually felt guilty about mistreating her granddaughter. Tears start forming in her eyes again. She gets up and creeps back to her room. Then she falls down on her knees, and starts praying.

Two Weeks Later

It's Saturday afternoon, and Billy Ray's friends are over at his house, playing. The three boys are stationed on the floor, having fun with Billy Ray's train set. Lorretta Lynn is thirsty, so she puts on her housecoat. It's still a little early, and she hasn't combed her hair. She doesn't want Billy Ray's friends to see her hair sticking up, so she grabs a head scarf and ties it around her head. She takes off down the hall, and all three boys look up and acknowledge her presence. She waves at the boys, and proceeds to the kitchen in search of Kool-aid. She pours a big glass and heads back to her bedroom. The little boys are still playing, and Sammy seems to have noticed her head. He waits until Lorretta Lynn is out of sight, and starts talking,

"Billy Ray."

"Huh."

"Yo' grandma must have a lot of money," Sammy says, looking over at Billy Ray.

Billy Ray continues to play, and says, "Unh uh, my Grandma don't have a lot of money. My Uncle Bobby bought me this train set."

Sammy stops playing and sits up straight. "I didn't say your Grandma have a lot of money because of this train set, Billy Ray."

"Well, why did you say that, Sammy?" Billy Ray says, looking confused.

"Well, I only said that 'cause I saw the maid walk to the kitchen. My grandma said only rich people have maids," He says, with a serious look. At first Billy Ray is confused, and then he remembers that Lorretta Lynn had just walked through to the kitchen. He jumps up and starts screaming:

"Get out of my house! Get out of my house! I don't want to play with you no more! My big sister ain't no maid!" Billy Ray picks up a train, and throws it at Sammy. The train barely misses Sammy's little head, and he rushes out the door with his other friend. Lorretta Lynn dashes into the living room to find out what's happening.

CHAPTER EIGHT

Two Years Later

Lorretta Lynn is sitting in her favorite high school history class. She's working on a school project, when Ms. Fitzpatrick walks over to her desk.

"How's that project coming along, young lady?

"Oh, I'm almost done, Ms. Fitzpatrick. You can look at it real soon," Loretta Lynn says, smiling and looking back down at her project.

"Oh my, I'm impressed. Maybe you can stay after class today, and I will look at it."

"Oh, ok. I'll stay over for a few minutes. I just have to make sure I get to the bus stop on time."

"Now, you know a school teacher is not going to make you miss the bus," Ms. Fitzpatrick says, as they both laugh, "I just want to look at it briefly before you turn it in. I'm sure everything is ok, though." Ms. Fitzpatrick makes her way back to her desk. This is one of her favorite classes, because it's small. This is the only class where she can give students a lot of individual attention. She drifts back from her thoughts and takes a seat. She notices Dennis has his hand up.

"Do you need something, Dennis?" She asks, looking over her glasses.

"Oh, I just want to let you know that my project is not done. Is it ok if I turn it in late?"

"I normally don't like to accept late projects, Dennis, but I am going to give you a chance this time. May I ask why your project is not done, young man?"

Ms. Fitzpatrick and Lorretta Lynn are staring at Dennis, patiently waiting for an answer. Dennis feels a little pressure, and almost wants to lie. He decides to tell the truth.

"Oh, I just didn't feel like doing my project," He says, with an innocent face.

"That's not a good excuse, and I may have to call your parents." Ms. Fitzpatrick's voice is stern, and the conversation is interrupted by the school bell.

Dennis is glad that he is saved by the bell. He grabs his book bag and jumps up. He responds to Ms. Fitzpatrick while walking out of the classroom, "I won't let it happen again, Ms. Fitzpatrick."

The other students grab their belongings and walk out behind him. Lorretta Lynn gets up from her desk and rushes up to Ms. Fitzpatrick. She hands over her school project.

"Thank you, young lady, let me glance at it so you can get to the bus stop."

"Ok," Lorretta Lynn is smiling at her favorite teacher.

"It looks good, young lady. I will examine it more and let you know if you need to make any changes. I'm very proud of you. Now grab your things so you don't miss the bus."

Lorretta Lynn rushes back to her desk. "Thanks for the compliment, Ms. Fitzpatrick. You are my favorite teacher," She says, with a huge smile on her face.

Ms. Fitzpatrick returns the smile and says, "Oh, my, most students think I'm too strict."

Lorretta Lynn is near the classroom door. "For real," She says, giggling, "Bye, Ms. Fitzpatrick." *If they think she is strict, they oughtta come stay with my Grandma for a while*, Lorretta Lynn thinks, as she makes her way to the bus stop.

Ms. Fitzpatrick is still in her classroom and she's thinking about Lorretta Lynn. Something just doesn't feel right about her student. She's felt this way ever since she met the girl for the first time. She drifts back from her thoughts and starts checking papers.

Next Saturday

"Child, you sho' been looking happy these days," Hattie Mae says, rising up from her rocking chair.

Lorretta Lynn is indeed smiling, while she's flipping her Old Maid cards. Hattie Mae is waiting patiently for her response. Lorretta Lynn looks at her, and bobs her head up and down. "I am happy, Grandma. I have a very nice teacher, and she always say really nice things about me."

"Sho' 'nuff," Hattie May says, while continuing to stare at Lorretta Lynn. All she can think about is how she had mistreated her granddaughter for many, many years. She's praying silently for forgiveness, and praying that Lorretta Lynn can't tell. She drifts back from her thoughts and starts talking again, "what is your teacher's name?"

"Oh, her name is Ms. Fitzpatrick," Lorretta Lynn says, shuffling the cards.

"Sho' 'nuff, sweetie?"

"Yeah."

"Well, she sho' 'nuff must be special, 'cause she's got a big smile painted on your face."

"Yeah, I'm gon' talk to her about college next week. I'm in the eleventh grade now, and it's time for me to start thinking about college."

"You been thinking about college for a long time. I can't believe you are in the eleventh grade, now." Billy Ray pipes up.

"I know. I can't believe I'm in the eleventh grade, either. Time flies. You are older, too, now," Lorretta Lynn says, smiling at her brother.

"Yes, I am. Still got a long time to get to the eleventh grade, though," He says, smiling.

Hattie Mae has started knitting again. She's wondering silently how Lorretta Lynn is going to get money to go to college. She doesn't have any money, and they all would probably be in a shelter if it weren't for Bobby B helping them. She drifts back from her thoughts and starts talking again.

"I sho' hope the Lord bless you with some money to go to college. Grandma is poor, and we wouldn't have made it over the years if it wasn't for Bobby B. God knew what he was doing when he gave me Bobby B for a brother."

Billy Ray is deep into his card game, but he loses focus when he hears his grandmother mention Bobby B. He loves Bobby B, and misses him something terrible. He looks over at Hattie Mae and starts talking, "Grandma?"

"Yes, child?"

"When is Uncle Bobby coming back over? We haven't seen him in a long time. I know you said he was sick," He says, looking wistful.

"Billy Ray." Lorretta Lynn speaks up.

"Huh?"

"It's your time to pull a card."

"Oh, I know...I was just waiting on Grandma to answer my question."

"Oh, ok," Lorretta Lynn says, "we been playing this game for a long time. Do you want to play Monopoly now?"

Hattie Mae takes a deep breath, and responds to Billy Ray's questions, "Child, I reckon Bobby B will be well soon. I'm sure this will be his first stop when he get back on his feet. Y'all not gon' ask Debra Anne if she want to play Monopoly?"

"You know Debra Anne don't like to play with us," Billy Ray says, looking down the hallway, praying Debra Anne doesn't hear him. A while ago, he wouldn't have cared if she heard him, but now he does.The whole momentum has changed for the better in the house, and he doesn't want to do anything to jeopardize that. Hattie Mae acts like she has a deaf ear, and just continues knitting.

The kids start playing Monopoly, and Hattie Mae is thinking about Bobby B. He has been diagnosed with liver cancer, and the doctors have only given him a few months to live. Hattie Mae is fighting back tears at her thoughts, when she hears Billy Ray call her name.

"Grandma?"

"Yes, boy?"

"You know the fair is coming. Do you think Uncle Bobby will be able to take us?"

"I don't know. Bobby B might be too weak to take y'all to the fair."

"Maybe he can at least bring us some money over?" Billy Ray wonders.

"I don't know, son. We might have to go into y'all's piggy banks for some money."

"Oh, ok. I almost forgot we have money in our banks," He says, pulling a Monopoly card.

The kids play Monopoly and cards for the rest of the day. Debra Anne comes out her room for a little while and then goes back. Hattie Mae hasn't seen Ms. Penelope in a while, so she walks next door. The kids turn the record player on, and start snacking on some chocolate ice cream and cake. When Hattie Mae gets home, it's late, so they watch T.V. for a while before heading to bed.

Next Week

The kids are all at school, and Hattie Mae is walking around the house, humming Gospel songs. She is getting older, and she's not getting around like she used to. She opens the living room closet in search of a hanger, and notices her mother's old cane sitting in the corner. The cane has been in the closet for years, but for some reason it stood out to her today.

Hattie Mae is in a daze while she's staring at the cane. She's reflecting back to the days when her mother was alive. She's visualizing all the times they sat on the fish bank together. She also remembers the times when they dyed and decorated Easter eggs. Tears are forming as she thinks about all the good times she had with her mother. She drifts back from her thoughts and closes the closet door. Hattie Mae walks to the bathroom sink and runs cold water on a towel. She looks in the bathroom mirror and starts wiping the tears from her eyes. Then she puts the wet towel down and meanders back to the kitchen. She opens up the kitchen cabinet and pulls the coffee grounds out; the house is quiet as she starts making her coffee.

CHAPTER NINE

"Lorretta Lynn," Ms. Fitzpatrick says, walking toward Lorretta Lynn's desk.

"Yes, Ma'am?" She looks up at her teacher.

"I looked at your project. You really did a good job."

"For real? Thanks, Ms. Fitzpatrick."

"You don't have to thank me, young lady. I'm always impressed with your work. You are a very smart young lady. I'm very proud of you."

"Oh, Ms. Fitzpatrick, you always say really nice things to me. I told my Grandma how you always make me smile."

"Oh my, you don't have to brag to your Grandma about me. I'm your school teacher. I'm supposed to make you smile, and help you be enthused about learning."

"Well, I really appreciate it. I told my Grandma last week that I want to go to

college."

"Well, good. We will talk about that briefly after class today," Ms. Fitzpatrick says, walking back to her desk. Dennis calls her name, and she looks back to see him with his hand up. "How can I help you, young man?"

"Oh, I just want to let you know that I completed my project."

"I was wondering if you forgot about it. Please bring it to my desk, Dennis."

Dennis gets up and walks to her desk. The class is quiet, because everyone is reading now. He looks over at the other kids, while handing his project to Ms. Fitzpatrick. He knows Ms. Fitzpatrick is strict, so he's praying she doesn't say something negative about his project. He stands there, waiting.

"Oh, you can go back and have a seat. I'm sure it's fine, Dennis. I will look at it thoroughly after class today."

"Thanks, Ms. Fitzpatrick."

"You're are welcome, young man."

Dennis walks back to his desk, and the school bell rings. All of the students except Lorretta Lynn grab their belongings and walk out.

"Bye, Ms. Fitzpatrick," Some of the kids call out.

"Bye-bye, I will see y'all later."

Lorretta Lynn is waiting patiently. "Oh, Ms. Fitzpatrick, I'm here because you said you wanted to talk to me after class."

"Oh, I remember, young lady. I'm old, but not feeble-minded yet," Ms. Fitzpatrick says, while chuckling and pouring a cup of coffee.

"You like coffee like my Grandma. She drink it no matter what time of day it is."

"Yes, most older people enjoy drinking coffee. Speaking of your Grandma, you said that you mentioned college to her."

"Yeah, I did."

"What did she say?"

"She said we don't have any money. Soooooo..."

Ms. Fitzpatrick interrupts her, "What do you want to be, young lady?"

"Oh, I want to be a lawyer," Lorretta Lynn says, with a shy smile.

"Oh my, I'm impressed. You're smart enough to be whatever you want to be. We will talk later. Get your things and run. The bus will be leaving any minute. I hope you haven't missed it. Come back if you did, I'll call your Grandmother and take you home."

Lorretta Lynn grabs her things and rushes out of the classroom.

Ms. Fitzpatrick finishes sipping her coffee, while trying to figure out what is going on in Lorretta Lynn's house. Lorretta Lynn is so different from the other students. They never like to stay after class. Lorretta Lynn always seems so eager and happy to stay over. Ms. Fitzpatrick starts thinking about their conversation. *Maybe I should try to finance her education...after all, I am getting ready to retire.* Ms. Fitzpatrick is very wealthy, and she had never had kids. She drifts back from her thoughts, and pulls out Dennis' project. She repositions her glasses and starts reading.

*****

Lorretta Lynn barely makes it to the bus stop on time, but she gets home and Hattie Mae is sitting at the kitchen table. Billy Ray and Debra Anne are both in their rooms. She puts her school bag down in the living room and walks to the kitchen. Hattie Mae greets her with a smile.

"Lord, you are beaming again today. I guess you had another good day at school with your favorite teacher?" Hattie Mae says, pulling hamburger meat out of the refrigerator.

"Yes, Grandma, I did. I almost missed the bus because I was talking to Ms. Fitzpatrick so long after class. I told Ms. Fitzpatrick that you and I talked about college," Lorretta Lynn says, smiling.

"Sho' 'nuff? What did she say?"

"She asked me, what do I want to be?"

"And what did you say?"

"I told her I want to be a lawyer."

"Sho' 'nuff?"

"Yeah, and guess what she said, Grandma?"

"What did she say?"

"She said I'm smart enough to be whatever I want to be," Lorretta Lynn is glowing like a light bulb.

Hattie Mae is silent, and she's fighting back emotions and tears. She is thinking about how she had mistreated her granddaughter over the years. She remembers the conversation she had with Billy Ray about Lorretta Lynn growing up and becoming a maid. She catches herself and drifts back to the present.

Lorretta notices her thoughtful state and speaks up, "Grandma? Are you ok?"

"Yeah, child, I'm ok. Just got sleepy all of a sudden. Well, we just gon' have to start praying that the Lord bless you with some money to go to college. Grandma just ain't got nothing," She says, fighting back tears and thinking about how Bobby B might not be around much longer.

Lorretta Lynn is looking at her, and she can sense her Grandma is in pain. She looks at her with compassionate eyes, and starts talking. "Grandma, I know you are on a fixed income. I'm gon' go back to my room and pull my school clothes off." She pecks Hattie Mae on the cheek, and Hattie Mae starts talking again.

"Yo' baby brother and sister mighty quiet back there. I wonder what they are doing?"

"Grandma, you know Debra Anne is always quiet. Billy Ray is probably taking a nap." Lorretta Lynn walks to the living room and grabs her book bag. She heads back to her room, then stops and peeks into Billy Ray's room. Billy Ray is taking a nap, like she thought.

Hattie Mae continues preparing dinner. She opens the refrigerator, and pulls out an onion. *Maybe I'll cook the kids some sloppy joes and french fries.*

Next Day

Hattie Mae is standing in the kitchen in her big house dress. She's warming up leftovers, and she feels weak as water. Mamie Lee has been on her mind a lot lately. Even though she's feeling bad, she decides to pick up the phone and call her sister. She lifts the phone, and then sets it back down. Her head is pounding so bad, she decides to get a couple aspirins. Hattie Mae pours a glass of water and gulps down two pills. Once again, she picks up the phone and dials Mamie Lee's number. The phone rings a few times before Mamie Lee picks up.

"Hello?"

"Well, hello, Little Sister...Child, you been on my mind so much lately. How are you doing?"

"Big Sister, I'm doing pretty good. I just been so busy with Buck, whereas I don't know if I'm coming or going. That's why I hadn't called you lately," Mamie Lee says, looking back at the couch to make sure Buck is still sleeping, "how are you doing?"

"I do ok. Just been thinking about you, and decided to call. You know the old folks use to always say that you need to call somebody when they keep falling on your mind," Hattie Mae says, chuckling.

"Yeah, you are right, Momma use to always say that. Have you been down to the nursing home to see Bobby B?"

"Child, I ain't been able to catch no ride. I shore got to get down there. The kids was asking about him the other week."

"Sho' 'nuff. I know they miss him more than we do. He's always been so good to them. Lord, the last time I went down, Bobby B was in bad shape. Big Sister, Bobby B couldn't even recognize me. I felt so bad, I left that place in tears. Lord, have mercy," Mamie Lee says, almost breaking down.

"He sho' 'nuff must be in bad shape if he didn't even recognize you. I gon' have to pay Ms. Penelope or catch a cab there. I'm gon' have to go when the kids are at school."

"Big Sister, do you even have money to catch a cab or pay Ms. Penelope?"

"Naw, I sho' don't, but I might just have to go into the kids' piggy banks. I'll probably find some money somewhere around here. You know how I like to hide money," She says, smiling into the phone.

"Well, let me know if I need to mail you some. I would hate for you to go into the money that our baby brother gave them."

"Yeah, you are right. I don't need to be going in those kids' piggy banks. They wouldn't have that money if it wasn't for Bobby B. I don't even let them go in their banks unless it's an emergency. Bobby B been good to me and these kids. There been time when I didn't have food to put on the table. I would get on the phone and call Bobby B, and he would come right on over and take me to the grocery store. One day, he noticed Billy Ray had a hole in his shoe. He put that boy in the car and took him to get some new shoes," Hattie Mae is breaking down. Mamie Lee just allows her to vent, then the phone is silent. Both sisters are trying to be strong, but after a few minutes, Hattie Mae starts weeping. After some time passes, she regains her composure and starts talking.

"Well, let me let you go, Little Sister. I know you got to go see about Buck."

"Yes, Lord. He just got up and went to the bathroom. Ain't no telling what he's doing back there. Lord, his mind is so messed up from this Alzheimers. Big Sister, just keep us in your prayers," Mamie Lee's voice cracks.

"Yes, Lord, I will. Love you, Little Sister."

"Love you, too, Hattie Mae."

They hang up the phone and Hattie Mae's head is really pounding now. The two men that everybody in the family could always depend on are both very sick. Bobby B is terminally ill, and Buck is plumb out of his mind. *Lord, have mercy. Lord, have mercy. Life twists and turns, life twists and turns.* Hattie Mae's thoughts are disturbed by a knock at the door. She is so preoccupied that she forgot it was time for the kids to make it home. She creeps to the living room and opens the door. All of the kids are smiling.

"Hi, Grandma!" They greet her cheerfully.

"Hi, chitlins. Y'all home, huh?"

"Yes," Billy Ray says.

"Everybody have a good day?" Hattie Mae closes the door behind the kids. Lorretta Lynn is glowing again. "Child, I can't believe you made it home with Billy Ray and Debra Anne. They always beat you home," She says, smiling.

"Well, Ms. Fitzpatrick let class out a little early, so she could talk to me about college."

"Sho' 'nuff, she still talking to you about college, huh?"

"Yes, and guess what, Grandma?"

"What, Sugah?"

"She gave me some college applications, too!"

"She did? Lord, I hope God bless you with some money to go to college. We gon' have to keep prayin'," She says, gazing at her granddaughter, and silently praying already.

Debra Anne had gone to her room, but she was listening to the whole conversation. Even though Debra Anne is very pretty, she lacks education confidence, and that affects her self-esteem. She despises Lorretta Lynn for being so smart, because she already knows that looks go away, but intelligence stays.

Hattie Mae makes her way over to her rocking chair. She's been feeling sick all day, and she felt worse after she got off the phone with Mamie Lee. Bobby B and Buck are heavy on her mind. She is jolted back to the present when she notices Lorretta Lynn standing in front of her.

"Grandma, you look like something is wrong with you," Lorretta Lynn has a worried expression.

"Yeah, Grandma not feeling so good today. Do you need something from me?"

"No, I don't need anything. I just noticed that you look sad," She says, with concern painted all over her face.

Hattie Mae loosens her throw blanket, and scoots up a little in her rocking chair. Her hair is sticking up, because she hasn't felt like combing it. Lorretta Lynn takes a small brush from the end table and starts brushing Hattie Mae's hair. Hattie Mae looks up at her and smiles.

"Thanks for brushing my hair, sweetie. I ain't felt good all day. That's the reason it look like this."

"You must have another headache, Grandma. I noticed your aspirins sitting out."

"Child, I got more than a headache. When you get old, you have all kind of stuff going on with your body."

"You not old, Grandma. Big Momma was the one that was old."

"Baby, you remember Big Momma? You wasn't much older than two when Momma went home to be with the Lord. You shore have a good memory," she says, glancing up at Billy Ray, who had just entered the room.

"Who is Big Momma?" He asks.

"Big Momma was my mother. You weren't born when she was alive."

"Oh."

"Grandma, you got manner in your eyes," Lorretta Lynn breaks in, "Billy Ray, get me some tissue out the box over there, so I can clean Grandma's eyes."

"Where is the tissue box?"

"It's right over there, next to the newspaper."

"Oh, I see it now." He says, walking over to the tissue box. He pulls some tissues out and hands them to Lorretta Lynn. Lorretta Lynn starts wiping Hattie Mae's eyes gently, and Hattie Mae is feeling guilty. No matter how hard she tries to forget the past, it always comes back to haunt her. Lorretta Lynn finishes cleaning Hattie Mae's eyes and starts talking to Billy Ray.

"Billy Ray?"

"Huh?"

"Go get my applications out of my book bag. I want to show them to Grandma."

"Where is your book bag?"

"Oh, I took it to my room."

"Ok. I'll go get them now," It doesn't take him long to grab the applications and return to the living room. Hattie Mae is grabbing her glasses so she can look at them. She has never laid her eyes on anything related to college, because she barely made it out of the eighth grade. She looks through the applications, then back at Lorretta Lynn.

"Child, I'm so happy for you. We just gon' keep praying that the Lord bless you with some money to go to school."

"God does answer prayers," Billy Ray says, smiling at his big sister.

"Boy, you sound like a grown man!" Lorretta Lynn says, giggling.

"Well, I know I'm not old, but I do remember when I was little, and I prayed for Uncle Bobby to keep his promise about taking us fishing."

"Oh, yeah. I remember that, too, Billy Ray..."

Billy Ray interrupts her and looks at Hattie Mae, "Grandma, by the way, how is Uncle Bobby doing? When are you going to take us to see him?"

"I have been wondering the same thing, Billy Ray," Lorretta Lynn says, and they're both looking at Hattie Mae.

"Maybe one day I will get Ms. Penelope to take us." Hattie Mae is feeling guilty about lying. She has no intentions of taking the kids to see Bobby B. She knows they wouldn't be able to handle looking at him. She doesn't have the heart to tell them, so she plays along. Hattie Mae decides that it's time for everybody to pray. Debra Ann is quietly working on a crossword puzzle, so they are all together.

"Let's pray, chitlins."

All of the kids are confused, and Billy Ray says, "Pray for what, Grandma?"

"We gon' pray for Bobby B, and we gon' pray that Lorretta Lynn get some money to go to college."

Billy Ray and Lorretta Lynn get up to sit directly in front of Hattie Mae's rocking chair. They are sitting cross-legged, waiting for Debra Anne to join them. Debra Anne stops playing with her puzzle, but she continues to sit in her chair. Billy Ray looks over at her and says, "Debra Anne, are you gon' come over and sit with us?"

"No. I can pray for Uncle Bobby right over here," She says rolling her eyes at Lorretta Lynn. Hattie Mae ignores her and starts praying.

"Lord, first I just want to thank you for being so good. It ain't always been so easy, in this little house made of wood. We ain't always had peace, and now it's finally calm. Thank you, Jesus. Thank you, Jesus. We got through the storm. We come to you today with a special prayer in mind. We ask you to heal Bobby B, just like you healed the sick and blind. We also need some money, so Lorretta Lynn can go to school. God, please hear our prayers and help us if you would. Amen."

The room is quiet now, and everybody is deep in thought. All heads rise, and Hattie Mae gets up to go to the bathroom. Overwhelmed is only a small fraction of what she's feeling right now. She finishes in the bathroom and heads to her room. All of the kids are still in the living room. Not too long after she closes her door, she hears commotion. *Lord, have mercy, Jesus...I just got through praying*. She creeps back to the living room area, and sees Lorretta Lynn and Debra Anne arguing.

"Grandma! Grandma! She just tore up my college applications! I'm getting ready to wring her neck!" Lorretta Lynn is chasing Debra Anne, who is runnning to her room. Hattie Mae starts hollering at the top of her voice:

"Hold it, hold it! Lord, we just got through praying! Lorretta Lynn, get back in here. Please don't go in that child's room!"

Lorretta Lynn turns around and slowly walks back to the living room. Hattie Mae is holding her heart like she's going to have a heart attack. Lorretta Lynn rushes over. "Grandma, Grandma, are you ok?"

"Lord, y'all gon' kill me! Y'all gon' kill me! I'm ok. Just let me sit down in my rocking chair," She says, while easing down in her chair. Tears are building in her eyes, and Hattie Mae is feeling guilty because she knows that she is the person who really created this monster. Billy Ray and Lorretta Lynn decide to give her some space, so they walk back to their rooms and close the doors. Hattie Mae grabs her Bible and starts reading; eventually, she falls asleep, and the entire house is quiet.

CHAPTER TEN

Ms. Fitzpatrick and a fellow teacher are sitting down in the teacher's lounge. They are sipping on coffee and eating their usual lunch. They are talking about their students, and Ms. Fitzpatrick is anxiously waiting to talk about Lorretta Lynn. She waits for Ms. Cunningham to stop talking, and then immediately brings up Lorretta Lynn.

"Oh, I have a student, and she's incredibly intelligent. I can just tell that one day she's going to be somebody," Ms. Fitzpatrick says, sipping her coffee. She sets her coffee cup down, and she's waiting for a response.

Ms. Cunningham clears her throat and starts talking, "Well, we all have some exceptionally smart students, although honestly speaking..."

"Honestly speaking, what?" Ms. Fitzpatrick says, trying to figure out why Ms. Cunningham cut off her sentence.

"Oh, what I'm trying to say is that, I don't care if they're smart or not. I'm nearing retirement. I couldn't care less at this point," She says, while looking at Ms. Fitzpatrick cross-eyed.

Ms. Fitzpatrick sits still, staring at Ms. Cunningham in disbelief. For as long as she's known her, she has never detected this side of her character. "Oh, my. That's not a good attitude for a senior teacher to have. I'm nearing retirement also, but I still care about my students. Matter of fact, I am thinking about financing Lorretta Lynn's education. My deceased parents left me a lot of money, and I might just invest it in her."

"Oh, my! You must really be fond of her. Is she a Caucasian student, or a...?"

"No, she's not a Caucasian student, Sara," Ms. Fitzpatrick says, looking the other woman directly in the eye.

"Oh, she must be Mexican, then."

"Well, believe or not, she's not Mexican, either. She's actually one of my Negro students," She says calmly, taking another bite of her sandwich.

Ms. Cunningham grabs her chest and starts coughing. Ms. Fitzpatrick doesn't say anything. She just watches and listens for a response. Ms. Cunningham finally regains her composure.

"Oh, gee, I almost choked. Did you say what I think you just said, Frances?" Ms. Cunningham says, looking as disgusted as anyone could look.

"Yes, I said what you think I said. My student is exceptionally smart, and I think her family is poor. She deserves a good education, just like any other white student, Sara."

Ms. Cunningham looks at Ms. Fitzpatrick like she is the scum of the earth. Before she starts talking, she turns around to see if any other teachers were paying attention to them. Once she sees that no one is paying attention, she blurts out, "Frances! You have made me lose my appetite. You mean you're contemplating sending a nigger girl to college? Oh, my. I mean, a Negro girl."

Ms. Fitzpatrick's face turns completely red. She's appalled, and is getting ready to let Ms. Cunningham have it. She straightens up her back, looks Ms. Cunningham squarely in the face, then lights into her. "What did you just say, Sara? Did you openly just call my student, a nigger? How dare you to say such a racist remark in this lunchroom!" She has rage painted all over her face. She knows all eyes are on them, but she couldn't care less. She points a finger directly in Ms. Cunningham's face, and lowers her voice to an angry, whisper tone. The whole room is quiet now.

"I'm demanding an apology from you! If you don't apologize, I'm going straight to the principal's office to report you."

Ms. Cunningham just gives her a look from Hell and doesn't say a word. Ms. Fitzpatrick demands an apology again. Ms. Cunningham raises herself up and pulls her glasses off.

"Let me tell you one thing, Frances. I'm not apologizing, and I don't give a damn if you do report me to the principal!

He probably feels the same way I do!" She jumps up and slams her chair against the table. Then she grabs her lunch pal and storms out of the teacher's lounge.

All of the teachers are looking, and they are trying to figure out what had just happened. Ms. Fitzpatrick is still sitting at the table and she's in shock. Suddenly, she starts having flashbacks about how racist her parents were; she reflects back to a time when they had gone to a hotel while traveling. Her mother left the maid a penny tip and wrote her this note: "Thank you, nigger girl, for your services. You ain't worth a penny, but I left it anyway." Tears are almost forming in her eyes, and then she's disturbed by a fellow teacher.

"Frances, are you ok? You just seem so distant right now," Ms. Pembroke says.

"Oh, oh, I'm fine, I just have a lot on my mind. Thanks for being concerned, Isabelle."

"Oh, no problem. I just didn't want to leave without checking on you."

"I appreciate you, Isabelle," Ms. Fitzpatrick says, trying to regain her strength.

Isabelle Pembroke walks away from the table. The other teachers have left the lunchroom, and Ms. Pembroke grabs her things and follows. Ms. Fitzpatrick starts to gather up her lunch, but one more thought crosses her mind before she gets up from the table. *I got to help Lorretta Lynn go to college, God. This is the only way I can pay my racist parents back.* Then she stands up and walks out of the empty teacher's lounge.

*****

All of the kids are getting ready for school. Hattie Mae has been feeling under the weather, so she decides not to cook breakfast. She removes the cornflakes from the top of the refrigerator, and grabs the sugar canister from the kitchen counter. She places both items on the table and then reaches for the powdered milk. She runs some water in the pitcher and pours in the mix.

"Y'all come on in here and eat. I ain't feeling too good today, so y'all gon' have to eat cereal and powder milk," Hattie Mae hollers to the kids.

"Powder milk?" Billy Ray shouts from his room.

"Yes, child. Powder milk. We ran out of the regular milk. Grandma is doing the best she can," She says, while thinking about how much she misses Bobby B. Billy Ray is the first one to make it to the kitchen, and his face is frowned up. Hattie Mae notices his expression.

"Boy, sit down and stop frowning. Don't you know some people out there don't have nothing to eat? You need to be counting blessings to God," She says, trying to find the strength to make some coffee. The girls make it to the kitchen, and Lorretta Lynn notices how weak Hattie Mae seems, and she sees how Hattie Mae is struggling with the coffee pot.

"Grandma, I have a few minutes before it's time to catch the bus. I can make your coffee today," Lorretta Lynn says, looking at Hattie Mae with compassion.

"Child, I didn't know you could make coffee."

"I only know because I been watching you make it for a long time," Lorretta Lynn says, grabbing the pot from Hattie Mae.

"Well, Grandma not feeling well today, so I'm gon' take you up on your offer," Hattie Mae chuckles faintly.

Lorretta Lynn continues fixing the coffee, and then she sits down to eat her cereal. She starts chit-chatting with Billy Ray, while Debra Anne eats in silence. All of the kids finish eating and they grab their lunch bags from the table. Hattie Mae is thanking God that she made the lunches the night before. The three children head to the front door and leave for school.

Hattie Mae closes the door behind them, then she opens the living room closet door. She's feeling weak, so she decides to pull her mother's old cane out. Mamie Lee has been on her mind all week. The two sisters don't talk or see each other much since Buck took ill. Buck's condition has gotten worse, so Mamie Lee decided to move back to Buck's hometown in Arkansas. Buck's folks promised they would help if she moved him back home. Mamie Lee didn't want to move back to Lutherville, but she felt like she didn't have a choice. Buck had already been diagnosed with Alzheimers, and now he has cancer, too. Hattie Mae's heart is so heavy.

Between Mamie Lee, Bobby B and Buck, she doesn't know if she's coming or going. She takes a seat in her rocking chair, and her Bible is planted in her hands. The elderly lady soon falls asleep.

*****

Lorretta Lynn is sitting in her favorite class. It is quiet because the students are working on an assignment. Ms. Fitzpatrick decides to walk over to Lorretta Lynn's desk and start talking in a low tone.

"Young lady?"

"Yes, Ms. Fitzpatrick?"

"I'm going to let class out a little early today. I have something I need to talk to you about."

"Oh, ok." Lorretta Lynn says, smiling.

Ms. Fitzpatrick walks back over to her desk and sits down. It won't be long before it's time for her to dismiss class. She decides to inform the kids that they can leave a little early today.

"Excuse me, students," She says, looking over her cat-eye glasses.

"Yes?" Dennis says, while the other students are just looking.

"I'm going to let y'all out a little early today. I need to speak with Lorretta Lynn after class. I don't want her to miss the bus, so I have to dismiss class a little early."

"Ms. Fitzpatrick?" Dennis says, while beginning to pack up his things.

"Yes, Dennis, how can I help you?"

"Is Lorretta Lynn your student pet?" He says, smiling from ear to ear.

Lorretta Lynn looks over at him and says, "Dennis, I can't believe you said that."

"Oh, I was just playing," He insists, before Ms. Fitzpatrick can respond.

Ms. Fitzpatrick stands up and walks over to Dennis' desk, smiling. "All of my students are student pets. Next time, I will just keep you over, young man."

"Oh no, Ms. Fitzpatrick, that's ok. I don't like staying over after class," He stammers, and Ms. Fitzpatrick tells everyone that they can leave. They smile at each other and he rushes out with the other students. Lorretta Lynn is still sitting and wondering what Ms. Fitzpatrick is getting ready to say.

Ms. Fitzpatrick walks back to her desk and motions for Lorretta Lynn to follow. Lorretta Lynn gets up and walks toward the desk. She's wearing a smile that is as big as a giant, and she takes a seat in the chair next to Ms. Fitzpatrick's desk.

Ms. Fitzpatrick smiles and starts talking, "Well, young lady, I have some really good news for you. Would you like some chocolate chip cookies before we start talking?"

"Oh, yes. I love chocolate chip cookies," Lorretta Lynn says, and Ms. Fitzpatrick passes her a few cookies and a napkin. "I thought I smelled cookies when I was at your desk earlier." Lorretta Lynn's smile is plastered on her face.

"Would you like a cup of milk, also?"

"Oh, sure, Ms. Fitzpatrick," She says, feeling incredibly special.

Ms. Fitzpatrick passes her a carton of milk, 'Well, did you get a chance to look at the college applications?"

Lorretta Lynn bobs her head twice. She doesn't have the nerve to tell her that Debra Anne tore up her applications. "I got a chance to look at my applications, and I also let my Grandma look at them."

"Oh, really? What did she say?"

"She just said that she hopes God blesses me with some money to go to college. She doesn't have any money to send me."

"Well, guess what, Lorretta Lynn?"

"Um, what, Ms. Fitzpatrick?"

"I have decided that I'm going to pay for you to go to college," She says, before removing her cat-eye glasses.

Lorretta Lynn is in shock and she's speechless. Surely she didn't hear what she thinks she just heard. She decides to get clarification.

"Um, Ms. Fitzpatrick, did you say what I think you just said?" Lorretta Lynn has an anxious look on her face.

"What do you think I just said, young lady?"

"You said you're going to pay for me to go to college..."

"Yes, young lady, I am."

"Oh, my God. Oh, my God!" Lorretta Lynn manages these words before getting up and jumping around the room. "Me and my family been praying that I get some money to go to college. Thank you so much, Ms. Fitzpatrick!" She has happy tears forming, "My family is so poor, and there have been so many nights when I laid in bed wondering what was going to happen in my life after graduation. Oh, Ms. Fitzpatrick. Oh, Ms. Fitzpatrick, thank you so much! "

"You are welcome! Get your things and run! I don't want you to miss the bus."

"Ok, ok...I can't wait to get home and tell my Grandma!" Lorretta Lynn rushes out of the room as if it were on fire. This is the first time in her life that she has ever felt so good.

Ms. Fitzpatrick gets up and closes the classroom door behind her. She walks back to her desk and sits down. She suddenly starts thinking about the conversation she had had with Ms. Cunningham in the lunch room. She knows she's going to be stigmatized for her decision, but for some reason she doesn't care. She had made a vow when she became a young adult that she would help a black person. Ms. Fitzpatrick had witnessed some ugly things that her parents did to black people, and it had always haunted her. Her parents left her filthy rich, and the only family member nearby is a male cousin. He lives in a town a short distance away, but their contact with each other is limited. She drifts back from her thoughts and starts checking school work.

CHAPTER ELEVEN

Lorretta Lynn has finally made it home from school. She spots her house and takes off running up the driveway. She rushes to the back of the house and bursts through the door. Her heart is racing, and she's almost out of breath. She slams the door behind her, then rushes to the living room. Billy Ray and Hattie Mae are sitting in the living room, and they can see that something has happened. They both start to panic as they witness her labored breathing and breathlessness.

Hattie Mae starts shouting, "Lorretta Lynn! Lorretta Lynn! What on earth done happened to you, Girl?"

Billy Ray is looking, and wondering the same thing. Lorretta Lynn just stands still while she's trying to catch her breath. Billy Ray is staring, and he's very confused. He knows something is going on, but deep down inside, he doesn't believe it's anything bad. Lorretta Lynn finally catches her breath.

"Grandma! Grandma! Guess what?!"

"What, Child?"

"Ms. Fitzpatrick told me after school today, that she is going to pay for my college education!" Lorretta Lynn says, while throwing her book bag down and jumping for joy.

Hattie Mae is listening, but she's in shock. She can't believe what's she's hearing right now. *A white lady going to pay for a Negro's education? Man, it must just be the Lord.* She comes out of shock mode and starts easing up from the couch. She grabs her mother's cane and starts shaking her head from side to side, "Lord, I told y'all chitlins that the Lord will make a way. Thank you, Jesus, oh, thank you, Jesus!"

Debra Anne is in her room as usual, and she is disturbed by the commotion. She opens up her bedroom door and decides to rush to the living room. She's standing like an outsider looking in. Nobody is paying her any attention right now, because they are all rejoicing and thanking God. Once she realizes what is going on, she walks back to her room. Hattie Mae starts talking to Billy Ray at the top of her weak voice, "Billy Ray! Billy Ray! Go put Grandma's favorite song on," She says, still shaking her head.

"What song, Grandma?"

"You know the song by Sam Cooke...'We're Having a Party'!"

Billy Ray rushes over to the record player and lifts up the top. He fumbles through the forty-five records until he finds Sam Cooke. He places the record on the turntable and cranks the record player volume up as high as he can. All three start singing the lyrics and dancing to the music.

The Next Day

The kids are getting ready for school, and Hattie Mae is creeping around the kitchen, trying to prepare a hot breakfast. Even though her health is failing her, she's trying to be a good grandmother. She realizes that she's made a lot of mistakes over the years, and she's trying to make up for it. When she finishes cooking, she walks over to the hallway and calls out to the kids, "Y'all come on in here and eat before the food get cold."

"Grandma, you cooked breakfast today? I thought you wasn't feeling good," Lorretta Lynn shouts from the bathroom.

"Yeah, the Lord gave me the strength to cook today. Don't worry about me. It's just my old age," she replies, walking back to the kitchen, aching in almost every bone. She fixes the plates and sets them on the table. When everyone takes their seats at the table, Hattie Mae looks at them and says, "Let's pray. God, thank you for blessing us with this hot meal and please bless us with many more. We also want to thank you for blessing us with Ms. Fitzpatrick's special blessings."

"Amen," The three kids say in unison.

Billy Ray and Lorretta Lynn are smiling from ear to ear. Debra Anne's face is blank, as usual. The kids eat their breakfast, before rushing to their rooms to grab school supplies. Hattie Mae is feeling weak, so she takes a seat in her rocking chair. The kids rush out the door, and Lorretta Lynn is walking fast. She passes Billy Ray, and he hollers, "Lorretta Lynn, why are you walking so fast?"

"Oh, I don't know," She says, giggling and stopping in her tracks.

Billy Ray notices Tommy coming out of his house, and he can tell he has on a new coat. He waits until Tommy comes closer, then he starts talking, "Tommy, I like your coat. When did you get that?"

"Oh, my uncle bought me this coat because I got all good grades on my report card."

"Oh," Billy Ray says, reflecting back to when Bobby B used to take him shopping. His train of thought is broken when he notices the bus pulling up. Billy Ray and all of the neighborhood kids jump on the bus. Billy Ray takes a seat next to his best friend and continues thinking about Bobby B.

*****

Hattie Mae is sitting in her rocking chair, attempting to read her Bible. Every time she reads a passage, her mind drifts back to Ms. Fitzpatrick's kindness. *Lord, I got to do something for this white lady. I don't have a lot money, but I need to show her how much I appreciate her. Maybe I can just put a fruit basket together and write her a thank you note?* She doesn't have as much fruit as she used to, because Mr. Fred has stopped coming over. She's been meaning to call and find out why he hasn't stopped by. The last time she thought about calling, she couldn't find his number. She decides to use the fruit that Ms. Penelope had given her last week. Hattie Mae creeps up from her rocking chair and slowly makes her way to the kitchen. She opens up the refrigerator, and pulls some apples and oranges out. She grabs a nice tin bowl, which had been given to her as a gift, and sets the fruit and bowl on the kitchen table. Then, she takes her notebook and a pen from the kitchen drawer.

Dear Ms. Fitzpatrick:

I just want to thank you for all your special kindness. I really appreciate you taking a special interest in my granddaughter's education. I thank God every day for putting you in my granddaughter Lorretta Lynn's path. As shameful as it is, I must admit that I mistreated my granddaughter for many, many years. The reason I mistreated her is because I despised her dark skin color. I constantly put her down, and you came and gave her hope. I made her frown and you made her smile. I told her she would never amount to anything and you told her she could be everything. I can't thank you enough for what you have done in our lives. I am sealing this letter with tears, and Lord, I don't know how much longer I will be around. If I leave this world before you do, please grant me a huge favor. Please let my granddaughter know that I loved her and I apologize for mistreating her because of her dark skin color.

Ms. Hattie Mae Russell

Hattie Mae cries as she places the letter in the bottom of the bowl. She grabs some Saran wrap out of the kitchen drawer and tears off a large piece. Tears are still falling as she place the bananas, apples and oranges in the tin bowl. She places the plastic wrap around the bowl, and seals it tightly with tape. After she finishes her task, she picks up the phone and dials Mamie Lee. The phone is ringing and she's waiting patiently. Mamie Lee finally picks up.

"Hello?" Mamie Lee sounds stressed.

"Hi, Mamie Lee, how are you doing? Your voice don't sound so good."

"Child, I been going through Hell with Buck. I started to call you yesterday, but it slipped my mind."

"Sho' 'nuff, Child, I know your plate is full. You stay on my mind all the time."

"How are you and those grandkids doing? I don't hardly get a chance to talk to y'all anymore. Lord, I got my hands full with Buck."

"Child, we just hanging in there. We sho' miss Bobby B coming around."

"Child, I know what you mean. I miss spending time with my brother, too. I sure hate that he is terminally ill," Mamie Lee says, her voice cracking.

"I don't even know how to tell the kids how sick he is. They keep asking me about him and I just don't have the heart to tell them. They know something big is wrong, 'cause he don't come around anymore. They don't know that the doctors have gave up on him, though."

"Big Sister, we gon' just have to keep praying that the Lord give us the strength to make it through this storm. You know, Momma used to always say, that he don't put no more on you than what you can handle. Sometimes I wonder, though," Mamie Lee says, her mind consumed with pain.

"Yes, Lord, you are right, Mamie Lee," Hattie Mae says, and waits for a response.

"Hattie Mae," Mamie Lee sounds distressed.

"Yes, Little Sister?"

"Hold on for a minute. Let me go back here and check on Buck," She says, laying the phone down. "Lord, have mercy, Jesus, Lord, have mercy!" Mamie Lee picks the phone up again.

"Mamie Lee, what are you saying 'Lord, have mercy' for? What in the world is Buck over there doing?"

"Child, I walked back to the bedroom and Buck was sitting there with his under pants pulled over his head. Lord, let me get off this phone. This man gon' kill me."

Hattie Mae is trying to say something, but Mamie Lee has already hung up. Hattie Mae just shakes her head and walks back to her room. She decides to take a nap until the kids get home from school.

When they get home, Lorretta Lynn goes straight to the kitchen because she is thirsty. The first thing she notices is the fruit basket on the table. "Grandma, whose fruit basket is this?"

"Child, I made that for your teacher, Ms. Fitzpatrick."

"Ooh, for real, Grandma?" Lorretta Lynn says, looking at the basket and smiling.

"Yes, Child. I don't have much, but I need to let her know that I appreciate her. My Momma always taught me that don't nobody have to do nothing for you. That teacher getting ready to spend a lot of money on your education. It's only fair for me to do something. White folks don't normally do too much of anything for color folks. This just prove what Momma used to always say."

"What did Big Momma used to say, Grandma?"

"She always just said there is some good and bad people in all races."

"Oh. Well, I can't wait to take her fruit basket to school. I know she's going to like it, Grandma. I see her eating fruit all the time in class," Lorretta Lynn says, before heading to her room to take off her school clothes.

Hattie Mae is stirring around the kitchen, looking for something to fix. Her food is rather scarce, because she doesn't have Bobby B to help her anymore. Bobby B stays on her mind; she had called the nursing home the other day, and they said he wasn't doing too good and might pass any day. She drifts back from her deep thoughts and pulls some spam out the cabinet. She opens the can, and then takes mayonnaise out of the refrigerator. Then she reaches into the bread box and pulls out some old bread. She's making sandwiches, and is happy to see some potato chips sitting by the sugar canister. She grabs them and puts some chips on paper plates with the sandwiches. She heads to the living room and calls out, "Y'all can come eat when you ready."

"Ok," Billy Ray and Lorretta Lynn say. Billy Ray heads to the kitchen and Lorretta Lynn follows. Debra Anne is still fumbling around in her room. Hattie Mae is feeling better, so she decides to work on knitting a blanket. Lorretta Lynn calls her name when she is reaching over to get her yarn and needle.

"Grandma?"

"Yes, Sugah."

"Do you think I need to put Ms. Fitzpatrick's basket in the refrigerator?"

"Naw, it will be ok on the table 'til tomorrow. Ain't nothing in it but some bananas, oranges and apples."

"Oh, ok."

The two kids are almost finished eating when Debra Anne finally makes it to the kitchen. She notices the fruit bowl and starts talking to Billy Ray. "Whose fruit bowl is that, Billy Ray?"

"Oh, Grandma made that for Lorretta Lynn's teacher, Ms. Fitzpatrick."

Debra Anne grunts and rolls her hazel eyes. Billy Ray doesn't say anything else. He just gets up and leave the kitchen, thankful that Lorretta Lynn had left before Debra Anne asked her question. Billy Ray walks into the living room to talk with Hattie Mae.

"Grandma?"

"Yes, Billy Ray?"

"Can I go down the street and play with Tommy for a little while?"

"Is your homework done?"

"Almost."

"Well, when you finish your homework, you can go. You can't stay too long, though, 'cause it is getting ready to get dark in a few hours."

"Yeah, I know. It won't take me long to finish my homework," He says, before rushing to his bedroom. Billy Ray sits on his bed and pulls out his homework; he works for around fifteen minutes, then heads back to the living room. Hattie Mae sees him coming and looks up from her knitting.

"Are you ready to go now?"

"Yeah, I am."

"Ok, remember what I said about coming home before it get dark."

"Ok, Grandma, I will," He says, before walking out the door.

Hattie Mae is knitting and watching TV at the same time. She's been feeling down all day, and she doesn't want the kids to know. She picks up the phone and dials Ms. Penelope's number. Ms. Penelope answers her phone after a few rings.

"Hello."

"Hi, Penny, how are you doing?" Hattie Mae says.

"Child, I'm doing ok. I ain't heard from you in a while. How have you been, Hattie Mae?"

"Child, I ain't doing so good. Got so many troubles going on. Bobby B is low sick, Mamie Lee had to move back to Buck's hometown,' cause he's low sick. Child, some days I don't know if I'm coming or going. Please just keep me and these chitlins in your prayers," She says in a pained voice.

"Hattie Mae, I know what you mean. Seem like when it rains, it pours. You know if anybody know about trouble, it's me. I lost my two siblings and my parents all in five years. They say the Lord don't put no more on you than what you can handle, but Lord, sometimes you begin to wonder, don't you?"

"Child, ain't that the truth. I might need you to take me to the market and to see Bobby B next week. I ain't got too much gas money, but I'm gon' try and scrape up something."

"Child, you know I don't mind, and don't worry about giving me no gas money. I know you are struggling trying to raise those chitlins. Just let me know when you are ready to go. That will get me out the house for a while," Ms. Penelope chuckles.

"Well, I sho' appreciate it, Penny. Let me get off this phone, so I can check on Billy Ray. He's down the street at Tommy's house."

"Ok, I will talk to you later, Hattie Mae."

As soon as Hattie Mae hangs up the phone, Billy Ray is knocking at the door. She gets up and answers the door. "Oh, I see you made it back. I was just getting ready to check on you."

Billy Ray is smiling like a Cheshire cat, and Hattie Mae is happy that he had some fun. "Go on back there and get ready for bed," She says, "you know you have to go to school tomorrow. Your sisters been in their rooms ever since you left. I'm getting ready to go back here and go to bed myself."

CHAPTER TWELVE

The Next Day

The kids have all left for school. Lorretta Lynn is on cloud nine, because today is the day she will be presenting the gift basket to Ms. Fitzpatrick. She was so excited, she almost walked out of the house without it; Billy Ray had to remind her that she was leaving the basket behind. The house is quiet, and Hattie Mae is stirring around in the kitchen. She's making her coffee, and glances at the spot where she had placed the fruit basket. She smiles and pulls her cream out of the refrigerator. She's suddenly disturbed by the telephone ringing, and she picks it up right away.

"Hello, this is the Russell's residence."

"Oh, hi, Mrs. Russell. This is Ms. Sampson from Safe Haven Nursing Home."

"Safe Haven Nursing Home?" Hattie Mae repeats the name, while silently praying that Ms. Sampson is not getting ready to say that Bobby B had passed.

"Yes, Ma'am, that's right. I'm sorry to disturb you, but I have some bad news," Ms. Sampson says, with pain in her voice. Even though she's been doing this job for a long time, she still has a hard time breaking bad news to families.

Hattie Mae is just holding the phone and praying that she's only having a bad dream.

"Mrs. Russell?"

"Oh, I'm listening, Ms. Sampson," She says, and tears are already forming in her eyes.

"Well, I just have to let you know that your brother, Bobby B, passed away in his sleep last night. I'm so sorry for your loss, Mrs. Russell," Ms. Sampson allows Hattie Mae a moment of silence.

Hattie Mae is weeping and asking God to give her strength. She finally builds up enough strength to start talking. "Lord, have mercy...I just had a feeling last night that my brother was going to be leaving this world. Lord, what am I gon' do? What am I gon' do, Lord?" Hattie Mae is breaking down on the phone, and Ms. Sampson just holds the phone and allows Hattie Mae to vent. Hattie Mae finally regains her composure, "I will call the funeral home and let the undertaker know. I reckon he will call you and make the arrangements to pick up the body?" Hattie Mae's voice is crackling.

"Please, let us know if there is anything we can help out with; I will keep you and your family in my prayers." Ms. Sampson says, before hanging up the phone.

Hattie Mae sets the phone back in its cradle for a moment, then picks it up so she can call Mamie Lee. She's praying, asking God for strength to just to make it through the day. The most important person in her life and the kids' lives is gone now. She's wiping her tears in between dialing Mamie Lee's phone number. The phone is ringing and she's waiting for Mamie Lee to pick up.

"Hello?"

"Hello, Little Sister, are you sitting down?" Hattie Mae says, while tears are rushing from her eyes.

"Yes, Lord, I'm sitting down. Hattie Mae, the nursing home done called me, too. What in the world are we gon' do without Bobby B?" Mamie Lee says, and they both break down, sobbing. Both sisters continue to cry and pour out their hearts to each other. Finally, they regain control and start talking again. Mamie Lee tells Hattie Mae that she will help her with the funeral arrangements, and they hang up so Hattie Mae can call the funeral home and Lula Bee.

Some hours have passed, and the kids have made it home from school. They all walk in the door and notice Hattie Mae's eyes are bloodshot red. They can't imagine what's wrong. Debra Anne goes to her room, while Billy Ray and Lorretta Lynn stay in the living room, searching for words to say. They are both looking at Hattie Mae, and Billy Ray starts talking.

"Grandma, you look like you been crying. What's wrong?"

Hattie Mae tries to brace herself before answering Billy Ray's question. For so long, she had hid that Bobby B was terminally ill. Now the time has come where she can't protect their feelings anymore. Tears are forming in her eyes as she prepares to break the bad news. Both kids are standing up, wondering what she's going to tell them.

"Baby, yes, Grandma has been crying today. I got some real bad news that I have to tell y'all."

"Go ahead, Grandma. We are listening," Lorretta Lynn says, trying to brace herself.

"Lord, I hate to tell y'all this, but..." Hattie Mae pauses, "but Bobby B died today."

Both kids start screaming at the top of their voices; Billy Ray starts beating the couch pillow, and Lorretta Lynn jumps on Hattie Mae's lap for comfort.

"Grandma! Grandma! Please don't tell us that our favorite Uncle Bobby died!" Billy Ray screams. He notices Debra Anne rushing down the hall. "Debra Anne! Debra Anne! Uncle Bobby died!" He shouts, running to his sister for comfort.

"Oh no! Oh no! You are lying, Baby Brother!"

"Uncle Bobby is gone! Uncle Bobby is gone!" Billy Ray is still screaming and clinging to Debra Anne.

Lorretta Lynn is in a fetal position on Hattie Mae's lap. All of the kids are crying hysterically, and Hattie Mae is calling out to the Lord, "Lord, help us all. Lord, please, help us all!"

A couple of hours pass, and the room is finally quiet. Tears are still falling from their eyes. The three kids are on the couch, holding each other. This is the first time that Debra Anne has ever longed to be embraced by her sister. Right now, they are so close, a bulldozer wouldn't be able to separate them. Their eyes are on Hattie Mae; all they want is some love and comfort now. Hattie Mae looks over at them and starts talking.

"Everything gon' be alright. We just gon' have to keep trusting on the Lord, and leaning on Him. Y'all's Uncle Bobby was tired of suffering. The nurse said he told her that he was ready to go home and be with the Lord. Believe it or not, he died the very next day. He ain't in no pain no more," Hattie Mae's tears start forming again.

Lorretta Lynn wipes her eyes, "But, Grandma, I'm getting ready to graduate. Uncle Bobby always told me he couldn't wait to see me with my cap and gown on. Now, he won't even be there," She barely gets the words out before she bursts into tears again.

Debra Anne and Billy Ray hug her tighter. They are all crying again, and Hattie Mae can feel their pain. She knows, as well as the kids, that life is going to be different now. All they can do is keep trusting in the Lord.

"Baby, he won't be there physically, but he will definitely be in your spirits," Hattie Mae says, "nobody in this house will ever forget Bobby B. He will always hold a special place in all our hearts. Lord, he was so good to us. He was so good to us," she chokes up, "it's time to pray...it's time to pray."

Everyone joins hands, feeling the same exact pain. They all pray, and then they head to their rooms.

*****

Mamie Lee is sitting at home. She's been crying all day. Buck is so sick, whereas he barely knows that he's in the world. Mamie Lee feels so bad that she can't be with Hattie Mae and the kids. She's been wanting to call all day, but she's trying to wait until the kids go to bed. It is finally late enough, and she decides to pick up the phone. She dials Hattie Mae's number and waits for her to pick up. Hattie Mae picks up on the very first ring.

"Hello, Russell's residence."

"Hi, Big Sister, how are you and the kids holding up over there? I know you had to break the bad news to them."

"Yes, Lord. Yes, Lord. I thought I was gon' have to call Ms. Penelope to come over here and help me with them. Lord, Mamie Lee, they took it so hard. Lord, have mercy. I feel so sorry for them," Hattie Mae says, wishing she was sitting in the same room with her sister.

"Child, I know they took it hard. They loved Bobby B, and he loved them, too. I feel so bad, because I can't even come over and see about them. Lord, my hands are tied with Buck."

"Child, I understand. I know you are tied down at that house with Buck. We gon' be ok, though. You know the Bible say, cast your burdens on the Lord."

"Yes, Lord. All of us need to do that. What are you gon' do about the funeral arrangements?" Mamie Lee asks.

"I'm gon' call Bobby B's old lady, Lula Bee. She told me some weeks ago that Baby Brother had given her his insurance papers."

"Ok. Let me know, Hattie Mae. I'm gon' call the nursing home right now and see if the undertaker picked up his body. I'll call the funeral home, too, and let them know you gon' get the insurance papers from Lula Bee."

"Ok. Mamie Lee, I will talk to you tomorrow." The two sisters hang up the phone, and Hattie Mae went to bed.

Chapter Thirteen

It's Saturday morning and it's still early. The kids are still in their rooms and Hattie Mae is piddling around in the kitchen. Her mind is in another world because of Bobby B's death. She knows she needs to call Lula Bee, but she can't seem to get the energy. Tears start falling from her eyes when she thinks about how many times she actually visited Bobby B. Her thoughts are suddenly disturbed by Lorretta Lynn's presence.

"Good morning, Sugah."

"Good morning, Grandma."

"What are you doing up so early?" Hattie Mae asks, already knowing the reason.

"I just couldn't sleep last night. I kept thinking about Uncle Bobby."

"I know what you mean, Baby. I didn't sleep that good myself. Bobby B was such a loving, good man. Everybody gon' miss him," She says, watching the tears build up in her granddaughter's eyes. Hattie Mae wants to give her a big hug, but it almost seems awkward. She had mistreated the child for so long, and her feelings continue to haunt her. But before she knows it, she has grabbed Lorretta Lynn. She hugs and grips her tighter than she ever has; Lorretta Lynn welcomes it, and they both begin to weep.

When they regain their composure, Lorretta Lynn begins to talk. "I am getting ready to go back to my room, Grandma, I feel really tired."

"Ok, Sugah. Just remember, we all gon' be ok."

"Ok, Grandma," She says, heading back to her room.

Hattie Mae picks up the phone and dials Lula Bee's number. "How are you doing, Lula? I been meaning to call you, but my mind is so messed up from losing Bobby B."

"I know what you mean, Hattie Mae. I don't know if I'm coming or going, either."

"Child, I just need to know if you still have Bobby B's insurance papers?"

"Yes, I have them. I was wondering if he told y'all I had them. Do you want me to bring them over?"

"Yes, Lord, if that's not too much of a problem. I know you are old like me and don't drive too much."

"Honey, you are right. I'm not gon' drive. I'm gon' get my son to bring me."

"Well, I sho' appreciate it," Hattie Mae says, wondering to herself if Lula Bee's son would take her to the funeral home.

The two women hang up and Hattie Mae walks over to the refrigerator. She's looking for something to eat, then notices Billy Ray standing and staring.

"Good morning, Sugah."

"Good morning, Grandma."

"How Grandma's boy feeling today?" Again, Hattie Mae already knows the answer.

"I had a nightmare, but I'm ok. When are we having Uncle Bobby's funeral?"

"Sometime next week," She says, looking at him with a warm smile.

"Are you cooking breakfast today?"

"Yeah, I'm gon' put something together. Ain't too much here, though. Ms. Penelope gon' take me to the market in a few days."

"What happened to the man that used to bring us fruit? He ain't been over here in a long time."

"Child, I been wondering the same thing. I been meaning to call Fred, but I misplaced his phone number."

"Oh. I guess I'll go back to my room. Call me when the food is ready."

"Ok, Sugah. I will."

Billy Ray is walking back to his room in a very sad state. Uncle Bobby was one of the most important relatives in his life, and he just can't imagine life without him. *It's bad enough that Lorretta Lynn will be leaving for college soon.* His eyes become watery as he enters his room and closes the door. He lays down for a short while, and then he hears Hattie Mae calling his name. *Oh, it must be time to eat*, he thinks, and heads back to the kitchen. Lorretta Lynn is waiting on him, but Debra Anne is in her room, crying.

"I smell toast," He says, pulling a chair from the table.

"Yeah, I just made some toast and oatmeal. I'm gon' buy some sausage and milk when I go to the market."

"Are we having powder milk again, Grandma?"

"Yeah, I'm afraid so. Put a lot of sugar and butter in it. That might make it taste a little better."

"Ok," He says, wishing he had some real milk.

"Where is Debra Anne?" Hattie Mae asks, while dipping some more oatmeal.

"I think she is in her room, crying," Lorretta Lynn says, with a sad face.

Hattie Mae starts praying silently, *Lord help these chitlins...please, help these chitlins.* "Well, I guess she'll come eat when she feel like it." She looks over at Billy Ray, and he is chowing down as usual.

"Tommy said the Wizard of Oz is coming on today," Billy Ray says, talking around a mouthful of food.

"Oooh, for real? That is one of my favorite movies!" Lorretta Lynn says, smiling at her brother.

"Yep, mine too. Maybe we can watch it together. I'm gon' miss you when you leave for college."

"I'm gon' miss u, too. We still gon' get a chance to see each other. I'm not going too far from home, and oh, by the way, speaking of college..."

"Yes?" Billy Ray is wondering what she is going to say.

"Oh, this is for Grandma. I forgot to tell you that Ms. Fitzpatrick really like that fruit basket you made. She told me to tell you thank you."

Hattie Mae smiles. "Tell her she is quite welcome. I wish I could have done more."

"Ok, I will, Grandma," Lorretta Lynn says, before looking back over at Billy Ray. "Billy Ray?"

"Huh?"

"What time is the Wizard of Oz coming on?"

"Probably around 3 or 4."

"Oh, I said I would watch it with you, but I forgot my friend asked me to go skating. Grandma, can I go skating?"

Hattie Mae doesn't say anything. She normally doesn't like for the kids to be too far out of her eye sight, but, maybe this will make her granddaughter feel better. She drifts back from her thoughts and says yes. Lorretta Lynn is excited and smiling.

"Thanks so much, Grandma. I'm sorry I waited to the last minute to ask."

"No problem."

Lorretta Lynn and Billy Ray get up and head to the living room. Debra Anne still hasn't made it to the kitchen. The TV is already on, and Billy Ray walks up to it and starts flipping channels. He stops when he notices the Three Stooges. He sits down on the couch and starts watching the show with Lorretta Lynn. Hattie Mae is in the kitchen, cleaning up breakfast, and Debra Anne is still in her room. Hattie Mae remembers that she never told the kids that Mamie Lee had moved to Lutherville. She finishes cleaning and walks to the living room.

"Did I tell y'all that Aunt Mamie had moved to Lutherville?" She asks, looking at both kids.

"No, Grandma, you didn't tell us. How come she moved?"

"Well, y'all already knew Uncle Buck was sick. Well, anyway, his condition got so bad whereas he couldn't even remember his name. He even stole Mamie Lee's car keys and left the house. The police finally found him and brought him home. After this, Mamie Lee decided that she needed some help. The only people that agreed to help her was his folks in Lutherville. That's the only reason she moved away."

"First, Uncle Bobby die and now Uncle Buck is real sick. What's going to happen next?" Billy Ray says.

"I hope we don't lose Uncle Buck, too," Lorretta Lynn says.

Hattie Mae purposefully changes the subject. "Child, ain't it time for you to be getting ready to go skating?"

"Oh, yeah, it is..." Lorretta Lynn trails off, her mind on overload. She gets up and starts walking back to her room.

Debra Anne is on her way to the living room now, and Hattie Mae notices her coming. "Girl, you didn't even eat your breakfast today."

"I know. I don't have no appetite, Grandma," Debra Anne says, her eyes red.

Billy Ray looks over at her, and can tell she's very sad. "Debra Anne, the Wizard of Oz is coming on today," .

"It is?"

"Yep."

"You gon' watch it with me?"

"Yeah. Let me just go in the kitchen and get some Kool-aid," Debra Anne says, heading to the kitchen.

Hattie Mae walks back to her room and picks up the telephone. She forgot to ask Lula Bee what time she was coming over. Lorretta Lynn leaves a few hours later, and the other two kids watch the Wizard of Oz.

CHAPTER FOURTEEN

Six Months Later

Hattie Mae is stirring around the house in turtle mode. Her whole life has changed since she lost Bobby B. There are many days when she doesn't even feel like getting up in the morning. The only thing that keeps her going is her grandkids. Buck is terminally ill now, so she hardly gets a chance to talk to Mamie Lee. Her health has become very fragile, and she prays every day for God to leave her on the earth until Billy Ray graduates. She's pulling some coffee out of the cupboard when suddenly she's disturbed by the phone.

"Russell's residence."

Nobody replies, but Hattie Mae hears profanity in the background. She decides to start talking again.

"Hello! Hello! Is anybody there?" Suddenly, she hears someone grab the phone and start cursing like a sailor. Hattie Mae is stunned once she realizes it is Mamie Lee.

"Mamie Lee! Mamie Lee!"

"Yes, Big Sister! Yes, Big Sister!" Mamie Lee's voice is hysterical.

Hattie Mae is getting worried, thinking that she can't mentally deal with more bad news. She calls her sister's name again.

"Mamie Lee! What on earth done happened to you? I ain't never heard you curse like this, Mamie Lee."

Mamie Lee is breathing so hard that she can't catch her breath. She is trying to talk, but she can't get the words out.

Hattie Mae is getting worried. She takes a deep breath and starts talking again.

"Mamie Lee, you need to calm down and tell me what happened. Lord, I can't help you if I don't know what is wrong!" She says, anxiously waiting for an answer.

"I'm trying to, Big Sister. I'm trying to..."

"Child, do you need me to send the police or ambulance over there?" Hattie Mae is holding the phone and trembling.

Mamie Lee calms down a little.

"Naw, Big Sister, you don't need to send no police or ambulance. I'm just real upset, that's all."

"Child, what are you so upset about? I ain't never seen you this upset in my life." Hattie May is dying to hear an answer.

Mamie Lee has finally regained her composure, and she takes a deep breath. "Child, you ain't gon' believe what I am getting ready to tell you." She takes a drink of what Hattie Mae assumes to be coffee.

"What done happened, Mamie Lee?" Hattie Mae asks.

"Lord, I was sitting on the couch, watching T.V.,"

"Yes?" Hattie Mae says.

"All of a sudden, I hear a knock at my front door, "

"Lord, ain't nobody tried to rob you, did they, Little Sister?"

"Naw, ain't nobody tried to rob me. It was a strange man standing there,"

"Strange man?" Hattie Mae is trying to figure out what Mamie Lee is getting ready to say.

"Yes, Ma'am."

"Well, who was the man, Mamie Lee? And why was he knocking on your door?"

"Hattie Mae, that SOB, he told me he was Buck's son!"

Hattie Mae thought she was hearing things. Buck had always told Mamie Lee that he didn't have kids. "Mamie Lee, are you sure he was at the right house? Buck ain't supposed to have no kids!"

"Yes, that's what I thought, too. I'm so mad, Big Sister, I don't know what to do! You ain't even heard the worst part!" "

"Hush yo' mouth. What you mean, I ain't heard the worst part?"

"I mean, he got a twin sister, and Buck got his mammy pregnant during the time he's been married to me!"

"Mamie Lee, hush yo' mouth! You mean to tell me, that that no good son of a biscuit had an affair on you?"

"Yes, Ma'am! Now you see why I called you, and why I'm so upset."

"Lord, please forgive my French," Hattie Mae says, her temper on fire, "W ell, I be damned! I always thought Buck was such a good man. I use to ask God all the time, how come He didn't bless me with a man like Buck. Lord, have mercy, I'm speechless."

They both remain silent for a few minutes.

"Yeah, Big Sister, I thought I had a good man, too! Buck wouldn't even look at a woman when we were together." Mamie Lee's voice is crackling.

The two sisters are quiet now. They are holding their phones, and they are reflecting back. Hattie Mae remembers when she found out her husband was having an affair, and Mamie Lee remembers when her mother said, "You don't know what someone is doing, unless you are following them around 24 hours a day." They both drift back from their thoughts when Mamie Lee starts talking, "Big Sister, I just don't know how much more I can take, I really don't," Mamie Lee has tears choking her voice.

"You gon' be fine, Mamie Lee, you gon' be fine. You never told me if you let him in."

"Naw, I didn't let him in. I told him to get off my porch before I put a bullet up his tail."

"Lord, have mercy, Mamie Lee, you know that wasn't right."

"I don't care if it wasn't right. I was angry! I slammed the door so hard, whereas it almost put Buck one foot in the grave!"

"Mamie Lee, hush yo' mouth. You suppose' to be a Christian. You ain't got no business treating that boy like that. He didn't have nothing to do with what Buck did in the streets. I think you owe him an apology." Hattie Mae scratched her head.

Mamie Lee is quiet. She's thinking about her sister's words. She knows Hattie Mae is telling the truth, but deep down inside, she's too hurt to accept it. She drifts back from her thoughts and starts talking, "Big Sister, I know you are telling me the truth, but I was mad. I guess I'm gon' have to ask the Lord for forgiveness."

"I know you are upset, but you never know..."

"Never know what, Big Sister?"

"Those twins might be a blessing in disguise."

"What do you mean by that, Hattie Mae?"

"Well, you know Buck is a sick man right now. You gon' need all the help you can get, Mamie Lee. Those kids might help you if you give them a chance."

"Big Sister, I hadn't even thought about it that way. You probably right. I probably need to try and get in touch with him."

"How you gon' get in touch with him?"

"Well, he hollered through the door, and told me he was gon' leave his phone number on the porch. Matter fact, let me get off this phone and see if I can find it. I'm gon' call him right now."

"I think that is a good idea, Mamie Lee."

"Ok, Big Sister, I will talk to you later. I love you."

"I love you, too." Hattie Mae says, and she hangs up the phone.

*****

Mamie Lee eases her way to the front porch. She starts looking around for the telephone number, and notices a piece of paper on the cracked porch swing. She picks the paper up and walks back into the house. She checks on Buck and sees he is still sleeping. She grabs the phone and starts dialing Fredrick's number.

*****

Hattie Mae has been trying to take naps off and on all day. Every time she lies down, she wakes up after about 30 minutes. Her heart is heavy, and her mind is clouded. All she can think about is that Bobby B. is gone, and Lorretta Lynn is leaving for college soon. She notices the time on the clock, and realizes the kids will be home from school at any moment. Hattie Mae takes some hamburger out of the freezer and starts fixing sloppy joes. She still has a lot of food that she froze from the funeral, and she's thankful that they can eat well for a while. She's stirring a potful of sizzling hamburger meat when she hears the kids at the door. Hattie Mae puts the spoon down and heads to the front door. Lorretta Lynn is smiling from ear to ear.

"Lord, there you go, showing off all of your pretty teeth again," Hattie Mae says.

"Yes, I guess I'm excited, because graduation is right around the corner."

"Yes, you right. I'm gon' have to dig in my closet to find something to wear."

"You can wear the pretty dress that you wore to Uncle Bobby's funeral, Grandma."

"Yes, you're right. I almost forgot about that dress."

Billy Ray breezes past Loretta Lynn and heads to his room. "Ooh, something smell good, Grandma. What did you cook?"

"Oh, I just warmed up some sloppy joes. I'm getting ready to open up some pork and beans, too."

"That'll work!" He says, closing his bedroom door.

Lorretta Lynn and Debra Anne head to their rooms to change clothes, while Hattie Mae is finishing up dinner. A few minutes pass; Billy Ray and Lorretta Lynn go to the living room and start playing cards. When the food is done, Hattie Mae calls them to the kitchen. After they take their seats, they all bow their heads while Lorretta Lynn says grace. Once the dinner routine is finished, the kids go back to their rooms. Hattie Mae makes her way to the living room to watch the 6 o'clock news.

CHAPTER FIFTEEN

Next Week

Hattie Mae is sitting in her rocking chair, feeling a little anxious because Lorretta Lynn is graduating this week. Mamie Lee is heavy on her mind. Hattie Mae hasn't spoke to her since Mamie Lee called, upset. She picks up the phone and dials her sister's number. Mamie Lee picks up on the third ring.

"Hello."

"Hi, Mamie Lee. How you doing? I ain't heard from you, so I decided to call," Hattie May says, feeling happy to hear her sister's voice.

"Child, I'm doing 'bout as good as I can be."

"Sho' 'nuff. How is Buck doing?"

"Well, we went to the doctor the other day. Buck is in bad shape. The doctor said it won't be long," Mamie Lee sounds like she's trying to be strong.

"Won't be long for what?" Hattie Mae asks, but she already knows the answer.

"Well, they say there ain't nothing else they can do for him."

"Lord, have mercy, Little Sister. Have you talked to his son yet?"

"Yeah, I told his son and daughter. They say they're gon' start coming over and helping me."

"Sho' 'nuff?"

"Yes, Big Sister."

"See, I told you those chitlins were probably a blessing in disguise."

"You sho' did, Big Sister. That's why I got right on the phone and called Fredrick. I apologized, and him and Fredricka came over the very next day."

"Praise God! Praise God!" Hattie Mae is smiling.

"Yes, it must be the Lord, 'cause nobody could have told me that I would welcome some kids that my husband got outside my marriage."

"Well, one thing for sure, Little Sister,"

"What, Hattie Mae?"

"You never know what life holds for you," Hattie Mae says, waiting for a response.

"Ain't that the truth? Momma use to say that all the time," Mamie Lee says.

"Yes, Lord. Momma may have not had a college education, but she sho' had a lot of wisdom and intuition."

"Speaking of intuition..." Mamie Lee says, looking back at Buck.

"Yes?"

"Remember how frustrated Momma used to get when I bragged about Buck?"

"Now that you mention it, I sho' do," Hattie Mae says, reflecting back.

"Now I wonder if she knew something I didn't know," Mamie Lee says, thoughtfully.

"Well, sometimes parents and old folks can see straight through somebody. I knew the joker Cookie was with wasn't no good. She wouldn't listen to me, just like I didn't listen to Momma about my good for nothing husbands," Hattie Mae says.

"Yes, Lord, old folks can tell sometimes. Well, one thing for sure..."

"For sure, what?" Hattie Mae says.

"I'm like Momma now. If you not following them around 24 hours a day, you really don't know what they're doing."

"Ain't that the truth," Hattie Mae agrees.

"Sometimes I can't help but to wonder if I pushed Buck to the streets."

"Little Sister, what are you talking about?"

"Well, I just mean that I nagged him a lot. And, not only did I just nag him..."

"What else did you do?" Hattie Mae says, curious.

"Well, a lot of times I wouldn't have sex with Buck."

"Lord, Little Sister, I didn't know that. You know Momma used to always say that you not supposed to keep depriving yo' husband of sex," Hattie Mae says, shaking her head.

"Yeah, I know Momma didn't raise me like that, but for some reason, I felt the need to use sex as a punishment. I was very controlling. Buck used to tell me that I wore the pants, and he was just my skirt tail."

Both sisters are quiet now. Mamie Lee's comments are too deep for Hattie Mae to comprehend. Hattie Mae drifts back from her thoughts and starts talking again.

"Well, I'm sure you thought you were doing what was best. I must admit that you are right, though. Sometimes we do push our men to the streets. I guess all us women need to realize that real men jus' want a women who can make them feel like the man that God created them to be. Although..." Hattie Mae pauses, thinking about her husband.

"Although what, Big Sister?"

"I just married a dog. I gave him sex, kept a clean house, cooked, ironed his clothes, supported his dreams, and he still went to the streets. At least Buck took care of your home, and he never brought his street life to your face."

"I guess you are right, Big Sister. No women ever called my home or disrespected me in the streets. Buck always made me feel like I was a queen, and I never wanted for anything. If I wanted a new car, Buck got me a new car. Same thing held true for clothes, too."

"Yes. Lord, Little Sister. Don't beat yourself up, 'cause you had a lot of good years with Buck."

"Yes, I guess you are right. Hold on. I think somebody is at the door," Mamie Lee says.

Hattie Mae hears a clack and knows that Mamie Lee has set the telephone on a table. A few moments later, Mamie Lee speaks into the phone again.

"Well, I gotta go, Big Sister. Buck's kids, Fredrick and Fredricka, have come to visit," There's a smile in Mamie Lee's voice, "I'm glad."

"Oh, Mamie Lee, are you gonna make it to Loretta Lynn's graduation?"

"I'll check with the kids and see if they can watch Buck. I hope I can make it, Big Sister."

Hattie Mae and Mamie Lee say their goodbyes, and Hattie Mae feels happy. She sits down and opens up her Bible.

Two Years Later

Lorretta Lynn is a sophomore at a small college in Mississippi. Billy Ray is in the ninth grade, and he's still living with Hattie Mae despite her failing health. Hattie Mae has been diagnosed with lung cancer, and she's fighting to stay alive. Debra Anne dropped out of school shortly after Lorretta Lynn left, and moved to New York in search of a modeling career. Buck passed away around the same time, and Mamie Lee died six months after him. Ms. Fitzpatrick retired, but she keeps close tabs on Hattie Mae and the kids.

Chapter Sixteen

Lorretta Lynn is sitting at an empty table in the student library. She's trying her best to study, but her mind keeps drifting back to Hattie Mae and Billy Ray. Lorretta Lynn is in deep thought, until she notices Trent from her criminal justice class. Trent is very handsome, and every time she sees him, she admires him. Trent is walking toward her table, and she suddenly starts feeling nervous.

Trent looks her in the eyes. "Hi, young lady. Do you mind if I join you?" He says, pulling a chair out from underneath the round wood table.

Lorretta Lynn blushes, "Oh, sure. Have a seat."

"Boy, you sure look like you're in deep thought. Is the lesson getting to you that bad?" Trent chuckles.

Trent's question catches Lorretta Lynn off guard. Studying is the last thing on her mind, but she doesn't want to mention that to him. She's concentrating hard on what to say, and she finally comes up with something. "Oh, this lesson is pretty intense. I've been studying so long, I now have a bad headache."

"Really? Wow, you must have really been busting your brain open. I know we have a test coming up in our criminal justice class. Is that what you're studying for?" He asks, with a look of confidence.

"Yes, that's what I'm studying for."

"Well, good for you, because I haven't even looked at the lesson," His smile shows all of his pearly white teeth. He pulls his corduroy tan sports jacket off, and places it on the back of his chair. Lorretta Lynn is watching his every move, although she's trying to be subtle about it. Trent repositions himself in his chair. "Well, since I'm here, we may as well study together. Right?"

"Oh, sure, I don't mind," Lorretta Lynn blushes again.

"Before we start studying, why don't you tell me where you're from?" Trent smiles, looking directly at Lorretta Lynn.

"Oh, I am from a small town in Louisiana. You probably never heard of it; we only have about five street lights in the whole city," She says, with a nervous laugh.

"Wow, what's the name of the city?"

"Homerville. Have you ever heard of it?"

"Well, I must admit, no," He chuckles.

"Where are you from, Trent?"

"Oh, I'm from Jacksonville, Mississippi. Have you ever heard of it?" He says playfully.

"I might be a country girl, but yes, Trent, I have definitely heard of your city."

They both chuckle and switch the conversation topic to the class assignment.

"So, what do you think is going to be on the test, Lorretta Lynn?"

"I think he's going to cover what we've been studying for the last two weeks. You know he talked a lot about the criminally insane trials."

"Yeah, you are right. He did talk about that a lot."

Lorretta Lynn picks up her pen and opens her notepad. Trent is very handsome, and she's trying not to stare at him too much. After she opens her notepad, she turns the text to the chapter where she had left her marker. Trent notices her turning to the specific chapter.

"What chapter are you on right now?" He asks, looking up at Lorretta Lynn.

"Oh, it's chapter 10."

"I normally study in advance, but I'm running a little behind this week," He says.

"Oh, really? Shame on you," She says, blushing.

He glances at the chapter a little and starts talking, "Well, I'm going to get out of here." He closes his book.

Lorretta Lynn is confused. She thought he wanted to study. She looks up from her book "I thought you wanted to study. That sure was short-lived." She smiles.

"I was just teasing you about studying. I noticed you sitting alone, and I decided to come chit chat. The reason I came here today was to make some copies," He says, grabbing his sports jacket. He puts his jacket on and stands up, "It was nice chit chatting. Maybe we can get together over the next couple of days, and study for real." Trent knows he is handsome, and he can tell that Lorretta Lynn admires him.

She takes a break from her book and looks up at him. "Oh, sure. I don't have a problem with that," She says, watching him pull a small note pad out of his pocket.

"Let me borrow your pen. I'm going to write your number down, so I can call about us getting back together," He says. Loretta Lynn hands him her pen. "Ok, spit it out."

"Oh. It's 602-132-5467."

"Ok, I got it. See you later."

Trent walks away, and Lorretta Lynn stares him down until he is totally out of sight. It is the first time she's received attention from a guy that handsome. She figures Trent probably only approached her because he thinks she is very smart. She opens her book again, but she really can't focus. This time, it has nothing to do with Billy Ray and Hattie Mae. She grabs her things quickly and leaves the library.

When Lorretta Lynn arrives home from school, she checks her mailbox as usual, and notices a letter from Billy Ray. She misses her family, and she's very excited about the letter. She rushes to her dorm room with the letter in her hands. Once in her room, she throws her book bag down, takes a seat on her bed and opens up the letter. She tries to brace her mind before she starts reading.

Dear Big Sister,

I hope you are having fun at school. Me and grandma think about you all the time. We really miss you. Grandma is very ill and she can't hardly get around now. She's on oxygen, because she can't hardly breathe on her own. I make cereal for us every day before I go to school. The neighbors come sit with Grandma when I leave for school every day. The nurse

*come over 2 or 3 times a week to check on
her. I want to join the football team, but I
can't because I can't stay after school. Well,
let me let you go. I know you probably have
homework to do. I need to go check on
Grandma anyway.*

Love You Big Sister!!!!
Billy Ray

Tears are falling from Lorretta Lynn's eyes as she finishes
reading the letter. All she can think about is Billy Ray
already having to be the man of the house. She visualizes
him getting up every day and preparing cereal for
breakfast. She thinks, *why does life have to be so hard?* She
folds the letter up and places it back in the envelope. She
puts the letter in her desk drawer and grabs some chips
that were sitting on her desk. The only consolation she has
right now is thinking about Trent.

*****

Billy Ray arrives home from school and notices an
ambulance in front of the house. He looks at the porch and
sees the screen door propped open. He can't hold back the
tears as he rushes up to the house. Once inside, he sees that
his Grandma is laying on the stretcher. He can tell she is
barely breathing, and the ambulance workers are starting
to roll her out of the room. Billy Ray starts screaming and
looks over at Ms. Penelope, who has tears welling in her
eyes.

"Ms. Penelope! Ms. Penelope! Please don't let them take
my Grandma! Oh, please, don't let them take her! I'm not
gon' have nobody now. Oh, not gon' have nobody," He says,
trying to go out the door behind Hattie Mae. The boy is
shaking while Ms. Penelope is trying to hold him back. She
finally gets a good grip and starts talking.

"Billy Ray, your grandmother is very ill. She almost stop
breathing, so we had to call the ambulance. She have to go
to the hospital, Baby, she have to go," She says, almost
breaking down in tears herself. Ms. Penelope is trying to be
strong for Billy Ray, but she's not doing a great job. Before

she knows it, Billy Ray breaks loose and is running behind the stretcher.

"Oh God, please don't let my Grandma die. Oh God, please don't!" Billy Ray is crying, and the ambulance worker is motioning for him to go back in the house.

Ms. Penelope is too weak to run, so she starts shouting, "Billy Ray! Come on back, Baby. Those workers got to get yo' grandma to the hospital."

The ambulance driver closes the back door to the ambulance, and soon the ambulance pulls away. Billy Ray turns around and starts walking back toward the house. Tears are pouring from his eyes, while he thinks about how everybody around him is dying. He stumbles onto the porch and Ms. Penelope greets him with a big hug. "Let's go pray, and eat us some good homemade cake, Baby."

The two walk to the kitchen and sit down at the table. Billy Ray is praying silently, while Ms. Penelope is cutting a slice of the cake she had made the night before.

The Next Day

It's early in the morning and Billy Ray can't sleep. Ms. Penelope spent the night, and she's sleeping in Hattie Mae's bed. Billy Ray feels so alone, and he's trying his best to be strong. Ever since Bobby B and Buck passed, he's felt like he needed to be the man of the house. There are many nights when he just lays in bed and talks to God. *God, I'm only a child and I don't know if I want to be a man...it's just too much pressure, God...it's just too much.* He picks up the phone and dials Lorretta Lynn's number. He figures she might be up studying her school work. He waits patiently for her to pick up, but Lorretta Lynn doesn't answer. Tears build in his eyes, and he reaches over for Hattie Mae's Bible, which is laying in her rocking chair. He opens up to a passage that his Grandma had marked. He starts reading, while tears are still falling.

CHAPTER SEVENTEEN

Trent and Lorretta Lynn have become very close. They often study together, and they have even begun going out to eat. Lorretta Lynn is very excited about the friendship. This is one thing in her life that she finds soothing right now. She prays every day for the friendship to move to another level. She drifts back from these thoughts and picks up her criminal justice book. It's been a long day, and she just wants to study and crash. She studies for about three hours and heads to bed. Suddenly, she remembers that she hasn't said her prayers. She jumps out of bed and falls on her knees. She starts praying for Hattie Mae and Billy Ray, and then she jumps back into bed. She falls asleep shortly after.

Early the next morning, Lorretta Lynn is already up, because she had a bad dream about Billy Ray and Hattie Mae. She sits up straight in the bed and can't think of anything to do but pray. She says a quick prayer and then reaches over for her criminal justice book. She starts reading and Trent crosses her mind. She knows it's too early to call him, but she decides to call anyway. She pulls her phone from the wall area and starts dialing his number. She anxiously waits for him to pick up.

"Hello?" A female with a baby soft, sleepy voice answers.

Oh, I must have dialed the wrong number, Lorretta Lynn thinks. "Ummmm...I think I dialed the wrong number. I'm sorry for awakening you," Lorretta Lynn is getting ready to hang up, when the young lady speaks again.

"Oh, who are you trying to reach?"

"I'm just trying to reach my friend, Trent. I'll just hang up and redial the number."

"Oh no, don't hang up. You didn't dial the wrong number. Trent is laying right here. Let me see if I can wake him up."

Anger flashes all over Lorretta Lynn's body, and she immediately slams the phone down. She sits straight up in her bed and tears start forming in her eyes. Her phone starts to ring and she's very hesitant to answer. All she can imagine is that Trent is probably trying to call her back. She slowly drags her arm to the wall phone to answer.

"Hello," She says, with a despondent voice.

"Oh, hi, Big Sister. Did I wake you up?" Billy Ray says, and he sounds sad.

"Oh no, Baby Brother, you didn't wake me up. I was just sitting here trying to study. You sound so sad," She says. Her mind has completely shifted back to her family.

Billy Ray is silent for a few minutes. Lorretta Lynn is praying that he won't give her bad news. Her day has already started awful, and she doesn't need anything else. She drifts back from her thoughts when she hears Billy Ray's voice.

"I just called to tell you that the ambulance took Grandma to the hospital. I tried to call you a few days ago, but you didn't pick up the phone," says Billy Ray. He is craving empathy.

"Oh my God, Billy Ray. How is Grandma doing now? Who are you staying with?" Loretta Lynn is trying not to break down.

"She not doing good, Big Sister, they had to put her in the Intensive Care Unit. The doctors say they don't know how much longer she's going to live. Her lungs are weak and she can't hardly breathe anymore. They have all kind of machines on her," He says, trying to be a strong young man.

"Oh, Billy Ray. This is so sad. Oh, this is so sad. Is Ms. Penelope staying at the house with you?" Loretta Lynn is fighting back tears.

"Yeah, she is staying here with me. She promised Grandma that she would take care of me if anything happened. We pray every day for a miracle." Billy Ray is struggling with his emotions.

Lorretta Lynn stands up and pulls the long telephone cord. She starts pacing the floor and praying. On one hand, she feels like throwing in the towel and moving back to Homerville. She hadn't felt this helpless in a long time. She knows she can't break down, though, because she has to be strong for Billy Ray and Hattie Mae. "Everything gon' be alright, Billy Ray. You know Grandma always taught us to pray, and that's just what we gon' have to do. We just have to keep trusting in God," She says, tears forming in her eyes.

"Yeah, I know you are telling me right. I'm older now and I'm trying to be strong. Some days it get hard though. It just seem like everybody I love is dying, Big Sister." His voice crackles with tears; he clears his throat and waits for Lorretta Lynn to say something.

"Billy Ray, I know it's hard. Our family have been through so many struggles. It seem like every time we get over one hurdle, here come another one. The one thing we have to remember, though, is that we always get through."

"Yeah, you are right, Lorretta Lynn," He says, "are you gon' come home to see me and grandma?"

"Yeah, I'm gon' try to catch the bus and come home real soon. Do you have the hospital phone number?"

"Hold on. Let me get it from Ms. Penelope." He hollers out and waits for a response.

Lorretta Lynn hears Ms. Penelope's voice say, "yes, Baby," in the background.

"Lorretta Lynn is on the phone. She want the telephone number to the hospital," Billy Ray says.

"Oh, just tell her to call 989-777-7777."

"Did you hear her in the background, Big Sister?"

Lorretta Lynn nods. "Yes, I heard her, I got it."

"Well, ok. I'm gon' get off the phone. We probably gon' be leaving to go see Grandma real soon."

Well, ok. Give grandma a kiss for me. I'll call you soon and let you know when I'm coming home."

"Ok. I love you, Big Sister."

"I love you even more," She says, before they hang up.

She places the phone back in the wall position. *What else can go wrong in life?* Family pain and now relationship pain. *Lord, have mercy,* she's thinking. She lays down in her bed and tries to fall asleep.

It's late afternoon now, and Lorretta Lynn is trying hard to study. Her mind is in a fog. Her stomach is upset and she's been constantly running to the bathroom. Trent hasn't called her, and she doubts that he will ever call again. She starts to reminisce about his good looks. Trent is tall, with caramel colored skin, and pretty, wavy hair. He has very nice teeth, and his smile can knock any young girl off her feet. She often wonders why he ever showed interest in her. She can't help but believe that it was all because she's smart. She drifts back from her thoughts and starts dialing the hospital number. The receptionist picks up.

"Saint Thomas General Hospital, how may I help you?"

"Oh, can you please transfer me to the Intensive Care Unit? I'm trying to check on my Grandma."

"Do you have your Grandmother's pin number, young lady?"

"Oh Ma'am, no, I don't. I'm away at college and I forgot to get it from my baby brother. Can you still transfer me?"

"I'm sorry, but due to our hospital policy, I can't transfer anyone without a pin number."

"Oh...ok," Loretta Lynn's voice is cracking, "I will just call my baby brother and get the number. Thank you, Ma'am." She gently hangs up the phone. *Oh, God, please just help me.*

*****

It's the middle of the week, and Lorretta Lynn is sitting in her law class. Trent should be walking in at any time, and she's waiting for him. It's been awhile since she talked to him, and she's hoping he doesn't skip class. She's in deep thought, when she looks up and notices him walking in. He's wearing a long trench coat and starched khaki pants. Loretta Lynn can smell his cologne as he approaches her area. He finally takes a seat next to her.

"How are you doing today, young lady?"

"Oh, I'm doing good. Did you get the message that I called?" She asks, while the law professor walks into the classroom.

Trent offers a half smile, and gently brushes her off, "Oh, we will talk about that later."

Lorretta Lynn instantly gets an attitude. She shoves around in her seat and accidentally knocks over her class books. Trent looks at her like she's crazy, and she starts talking again. "Can we please just meet in the Student Union after class, Trent?"

"Not sure. Let me think about it."

"Uh...ok," She snaps.

Trent notices her attitude, and decides to get up and move to another seat in the back of the room. Lorretta Lynn is stunned, although she tries to play it cool in front of her classmates. The professor, Mr. Frost, starts teaching. Listening is the last thing on her mind, but she reprograms her thoughts and tries to jump into the lecture.

*****

Billy Ray and Ms. Penelope are driving to the hospital. Billy Ray is feeling anxious, because he knows his Grandma is in bad shape. Ms. Penelope makes it to the hospital and pulls into the visitors' parking lot. Billy Ray notices that she passed a parking space.

"Ms. Penelope, we just passed a parking space."

"I know, Baby, but I'm trying to find a closer one. My legs are bad, so I can't walk too far," Ms. Penelope says, smiling at him.

"Oh, ok. I didn't know, Ms. Penelope," He says, thinking that it must be challenging to be old.

"Oh, that's ok. I think I see one right up there."

"Yeah, you are right. I see it, too."

Mrs. Penelope slowly pulls into the spot and parks her car. As they start walking toward the hospital entrance, Billy Ray is silently praying that his grandmother is doing better. Even though they had been through some stormy times, he always remembers how she taught him to pray. He's deep in thought when he hears Ms. Penelope calling his name.

"Yes, Ma'am?"

"Are you ok? We almost to the ICU area," Ms. Penelope offers a warm smile.

"Yeah." It's all he can say. He's trying to be strong, as usual. They finally make it to the ICU desk.

"Hi, can I help you Ma'am?" The nurse looks at Ms. Penelope.

"Yeah, we are here to see Mrs. Hattie Mae Russell."

"Ok. Y'all can go on back for a few minutes. Oh, wait a minute, Ma'am, are you a family member?"

Ms. Penelope doesn't like to lie, but she feels pressured to do so today. She looks at the nurse directly, and says, "Yes, Ma'am, and this is her grandson."

"Ok. Go on back, Ma'am."

Ms. Penelope and Billy Ray start walking to Hattie Mae's room. Hattie Mae looks like she has every tube in the hospital on her. Words can't describe how Billy Ray is feeling right now. Tears start welling in his eyes, and he starts whispering to Ms. Penelope.

"Do you think she know we are here, Ms. Penelope?"

"Oh, I don't know, sweetie. Why don't you try grabbing her hand and tell her to squeeze your hand if she can hear you?"

"Oh, ok," He says, gently touching Hattie Mae's hand, "Grandma, squeeze my hand if you can hear me talking." He is using a soft voice. Hattie Mae squeezes his hand, and tears start falling from his eyes.

"Grandma, I love you, and Lorretta Lynn say to tell you she love you, too," Billy Ray says, gently releasing her hand. He looks over at Ms. Penelope and smiles slightly. Ms. Penelope returns his smile, but doesn't say a word. She's trying her best to be strong for the child. Billy Ray starts talking again.

"Ms. Penelope, I hate to ask you this?"

"You hate to ask me what, sweetie?"

"Oh, I was just wondering if you have some money? I want to go to the gift shop and buy my Grandma a card." He looks at his Grandma with a sober expression.

"Baby, you don't have to be afraid to ask me for some money." Ms. Penelope reaches into her pocket book. She pulls out a couple of dollars and hands them to Billy Ray.

"Thank you, Ms. Penelope. Is it ok for me to go to the gift shop?"

"Yeah, go ahead. It's time for us to leave the room, anyway. We can only stay so many minutes on the hour."

"Oh, ok. I'm going right now."

He leaves the room and heads toward the elevator, noticing all of the sick people around him. He makes it to the elevator and pushes the button for the first floor. The elevator dings, so he steps off and heads to the gift shop. His mind is in turmoil as he searches for a card. His thoughts are disturbed by an elderly lady.

"Can I help you with anything, young man?"

"Oh, I'm just looking to get my Grandma a card."

"There's some cards right over there for grandmothers." She indicates a corner of the store.

"Ok. Thank you, Ma'am."

He walks over and starts looking through the cards. When he spots one he likes, he takes it off of the shelf and walks over to the cash register. He pulls two dollars out of his pocket, but the lady pushes his hand back and starts talking.

"Oh, don't worry about paying for the card today, young man. I have some extra money. I'll pay for it, ok?" She notices the pain on Billy Ray's face.

He looks at her with a sad smile. "Oh, thank you so much, Ma'am. Do you have an ink pen that I can use?"

"Sure, I have an ink pen," She grabs the pen sitting next to the register and hands it to him.

Billy Ray signs the card with his name, Lorrettta Lynn's name, and Debra Anne's name, with love. He puts the card in the envelope and writes "Grandma" on the front. He hands the pen back to the clerk.

"Thank you so much, Ma'am," He says, while heading out of the shop.

"You are welcome, young man." She replies, feeling sorry for the child.

Billy Ray heads toward the elevator, and he's silently praying. He's praying that his grandmother's eyes will open, but he knows, deep down inside, that they probably will not.

*****

Lorretta Lynn is in her room, packing her clothes. She promised Billy Ray that she was coming home for the weekend, and she isn't about to back out. She had asked Trent to take her to the bus station, but he said he couldn't, due to prior obligations. Trent has really been avoiding her, but for some reason, she can't get him off of her mind. She finally finishes packing, and heads to the bus station. She's feeling very excited, because it's been a while since she's seen Billy Ray and Hattie Mae. She makes it to the bus station and waits. When the bus pulls up, she jumps on and starts praying silently. After she prays, she pulls out a school book and begins reading. Soon, the bus is pulling into her small home town. She looks over to the other side of the street and notices a cab. Loretta Lynn rushes to the cab and starts talking to the cab driver.

"Oh, hi, Mister. Do you think you can take me to the hospital to see my Grandmother? I don't have a lot of money, but I really need to see her. She's in the Intensive Care Unit," she says, with such a pitiful look.

"How much do you have, young lady?" The cab driver looks at her desperate expression.

"Oh, I only have a few dollars. I am a poor college student."

He hesitates, and then motions for her to get in the cab. She jumps in and he starts driving. They make it to the hospital entrance, and she notices Billy Ray and Ms. Penelope walking out. Billy Ray is crying hysterically, and Ms. Penelope is hugging him and crying. Lorretta Lynn screams, "Stop! Stop! That's my little brother over there!"

The cab driver brakes, and Loretta Lynn jumps out of the car. She runs over to Billy Ray and starts shouting:

"Where's Grandma? Where's Grandma, Billy Ray?"

"Grandma's gone, Big Sister! Grandma is gone!" Billy Ray cries, and Loretta Lynn embraces him.

Lorretta Lynn starts sobbing, and Ms. Penelope puts one arm around Loretta Lynn's shoulder, and the other arm around Billy Ray. All three start walking toward the visitor lot, while other people are watching. Everyone in their presence can sense that someone special has died. When they get into the old car, Lorretta Lynn is screaming, "Oh God, please tell me I'm having a nightmare. Oh please, just let this be a nightmare!" She is repeating herself, and Billy Ray is in the back seat, sobbing.

CHAPTER EIGHTEEN

Six Months Later

It's a new college semester, and Loretta Lynn has left the dorm. She moved to a tiny apartment, so she could accommodate Billy Ray. Debra Anne is still in New York, and she doesn't have much contact with her siblings. Ms. Fitzpatrick is still in their lives, and she has really stepped up to the plate. Loretta Lynn and Billy Ray both talk to her on a regular basis.

"Hi, Big Sister. I wasn't expecting you home so soon," Billy Ray looks up as Loretta Lynn enters the apartment.

"Oh, I had a rough day, so I decided to skip my class."

"You must have really had a bad day. I can't believe you skipped class," Billy Ray is smiling.

"Yeah, it was pretty rough, but I have an A average, so I can afford to skip every now and then."

"Oh, ok."

"What are you up to? Have you started your homework yet?"

"I just got through eating a peanut butter and jelly sandwich. I am getting ready to do my homework now."

"Well, you know you are a junior now, and I expect you to get good grades."

"Yeah, I know."

"Well, I was just reminding you," She says, and they both smile.

"Well, let me go on in here and start my homework" Billy Ray says.

"Yeah, I am getting ready to go to my room, since I have homework, too," She says. She's doesn't want to tell him that she is feeling depressed. Trent is still avoiding her, and she can't seem to get him out of her system. Homework is the last thing on her mind. She walks to her room and closes the door.

A few hours have passed, and they are still in their tiny rooms. Billy Ray is tired of working on his project, so he decides to pick up the phone and call his friend, Lance. The phone rings a few times, and Lance picks up.

"What's up, Dog?" Billy Ray says.

"Ain't nothing up, Man. I just got through talking to my mom about possibly trying out for the football team," Lance says.

"For real? I wanted to play football when I was back home, but I couldn't because my Grandma got real sick," Billy Ray is reflecting back to when his Grandma was living.

"Well, Man, maybe we can try out together. I didn't know you were interested in playing."

"Yeah, I am, but my sister is not so keen on people playing sports. She seem to think you don't focus on your studies as much when you play sports. My sister is a real stickler when it comes to education."

"Wow. Well, just tell her I will keep you on track. I'll make sure you keep your grades up."

"Yeah, right, Lance. Like you really is somebody," Billy Ray says, and they both laugh.

"Well, you never know. Just check with her anyway, man."

"Yeah, you are right Lance. I guess it won't hurt anything."

"Ok, Man. Well, I gotta go. My mom is calling me," Lance says, and Billy Ray can hear him yell "I'm coming" to his Mom.

"Ok, Man. I will holler at you later." Billy Ray hangs up the phone.

Lorretta Lynn is still in her room, and she's really trying to study. Every time she attempts to read something, Trent pops up in her mind. She knows deep down inside that Trent is no longer interested in her. She's having a hard time letting go, because she has never dated a guy like him. He's handsome and has a fun personality. She drifts back from her thoughts when she hears Billy Ray knocking on her door.

"Come on in. What's up?"

"Oh, I just have something to ask you?"

"Oh, really? Spit it out," She says, smiling at her brother.

"I was just wondering if I can try out for the football team."

"Try out for what?'" She gets a very serious expression.

"Big Sister, you know you heard me. Football." He says, smiling.

"Billy Ray, you know I'm not a fan of you playing sports, right?"

"Yeah, but I have been wanting to play for a long time. Remember, I wanted to play when I was with Grandma, but she got sick and then I couldn't play."

Lorretta Lynn is feeling guilty; she knows what he's saying is true. Billy Ray keeps talking.

"My friend, Lance, his mother gon' probably let him play."

"Boy, I'm not your best friend's mother, and what does that have to do with us?"

Billy Ray gets quiet. He knows not to talk back or say anything smart to Lorretta Lynn. He wouldn't want to anyway, because he respects her so much. He drifts back from his thoughts when she starts talking.

"Well, let me just think about it for a while, ok?"

"Ok."

Billy Ray closes her door, and she starts looking for a classmate's number. *Decisions, decisions,* Lorretta Lynn thinks.

*****

Lorretta Lynn is sitting in class, waiting for Trent to arrive. She's praying silently that he pays her some attention today. She looks up, and he's walking in the door. He is looking good and smelling good, as usual. She's feeling nervous as he approaches her area.

"How are you doing, young lady?"

"Oh, I am doing ok," She says, while her heart is pounding, "what about you?"

"Oh, I am fine. I'm not sure what your schedule is, but we need to talk." He has a very serious look.

"Oh, ok, well, maybe I can meet you in the student union after class," She says, while the professor enters the classroom.

"Ok, cool." He says, and then walks to the opposite side of the room.

Lorretta Lynn's thoughts are racing. *He has never sat so far away from me. I wonder what he is going to say after class. I guess today he will officially end our relationship.* She drifts back when the law professor starts talking. She's trying to focus, but her mind is a thousand miles away. She sits in class for an hour before the professor dismisses it. She notices Trent rushing out while she's trying to pack her bags. Loretta Lynn walks out shortly after him, and heads to the Student Union. She walks in, and Trent notices her looking like she lost her best friend. He motions for her to come to his table. When she sits down, he starts talking.

"Hi, you look like you have a lot on your mind. Go ahead and get comfortable in your seat," He says, feeling guilty about what he is getting ready to do.

"Oh...oh...I'm ok. I'm ok," She says, with a nervous laugh.

"Ok. Well, um, I have been thinking a lot about our relationship lately."

"Umm...really..." Loretta Lynn's stomach is turning.

"Yes, really. Well, you see, you are a really nice girl, but..."

"But what?" She is silently praying for strength.

"Well, you are a nice girl, but I am not in...love with you, Loretta Lynn. I love you as a person, but I'm just not in love with you. I have been thinking about it lately, and I just feel you deserve better," He says, feeling terrible about what he is doing. Loretta Lynn has told him all about her past, and he knows being hurt again is the last thing she needs in her life right now. He drifts back from his thoughts when she starts talking.

"But, Trent, we have so much fun together. I thought we were really compatible. We both like the same things, we make each other laugh, we both want to be attorneys, we both even have really strong family ties and beliefs." Lorretta Lynn is trying not to break down in the Student Union.

"Well, see, Loretta Lynn, you are right. You are really right about the strong family ties and beliefs. Actually, that is one of my main problems."

"What do you mean, Trent?" Loretta Lynn says, feeling confused.

Trent clears his throat; he's trying hard to spare her feelings. He knows this girl is the last person in the world who needs to be rejected and hurt again. He musters up the strength, and looks around the Student Union to see if all eyes were on them. He's trying to find the courage, but she speaks first.

"Trent, I asked you a question. What do you mean?"

"Well, I hate to say this, but I have to say it, baby doll. Everybody in my family is light skinned. I'm actually darker than everybody. You are the first dark skinned girl that I ever dated, and I really thought I could get past your skin color," He says, while silently praying to God for forgiveness for hurting someone he really cared about, "Loretta Lynn, I tried, I really did try. I even showed my family a picture of you."

"And what did they say?" She is fighting back tears, flashing back to how her grandmother and sister had treated her for years.

"Well, they just said that you would never be welcomed into our family." He says, feeling like the lowest scum on earth. Loretta Lynn is quiet, and tears are falling now. She puts her head down and places her hands over her eyes. *Oh, God, not again. Oh, not again.* She jolts back from her thoughts when she hears Trent's voice.

"I have to go now. Take care of yourself. I'm sorry, Loretta Lynn," His voice cracks a little. He gets up from the table and tries to act like nothing has happened. He exits the Student Union while Loretta Lynn and other students are watching him. Loretta Lynn finally regains her composure and stands up. She walks out like she is the only one in the Student Union. Her biggest nightmare about rejection has happened, again. She prays silently, and heads out to catch the bus.

*****

Billy Ray and Lance are walking home from school. Football tryouts are next week, and Billy Ray is still waiting on Loretta Lynn's approval. Lance decides to bring up the subject, since Billy Ray hadn't said anything about it.

"Man, do you think your big sister is going to let you try out?"

"I sure hope so, Man. But, I really don't know."

"Well, let's keep our fingers crossed. I would love to play on the same team with you," Lance says, with a funny look on his face.

"Yeah, I feel the same way, Man." Billy Ray says.

They hi-five each other and head in opposite directions.

"See you later, man!" Lance says, stopping and staring at Billy Ray.

"Ok. Later, man."

When Billy Ray arrives home, he remembers that he needs to check the mail. He opens up the box, and sees a letter from Debra Anne. He's very surprised, because they haven't heard from her in a long time. Once inside the apartment, he heads straight to Loretta Lynn's room with the letter. He figures she isn't home yet, but he still knocks on her bedroom door. She doesn't answer, so he opens the door and places the letter on her bed. He shuts her bedroom door and heads to the refrigerator. He pulls out the Kool-aid and pours a glass. Loretta Lynn walks in shortly after, and he can tell she's had another rough day. He looks her up and down, and starts talking.

"Man, Big Sister, you look more tired than you did the last time. What's up with you?" He says, with a concerned look.

"Yeah, it's been a very long day and I have a lot of exams to study for," She says, not wanting to share the real deal.

"Oh. I can tell something is up. By the way, Debra Anne wrote you a letter. I put it on your bed."

"Oh, for real? I haven't talked to her since Grandma died," She says, feeling anxious to read the letter. *Maybe something in the letter will make me feel better.*

"Yeah, I know, it's been a long time. By the way..."

"By the way what, Billy Ray?" She is not in the mood to be a parent today.

"Oh, I was just wondering if you are going to let me try out for the football team."

"I'm sorry, I was supposed to get back with you about that, wasn't I?"

"Yes, but it's not too late," Billy Ray is smiling.

"Ok, Billy Ray, it's like this,"

"Like what, Big Sister?"

"I will let you try out under one condition."

"And what is that condition, Big Sister?"

"You have to maintain a 3.5 grade point average."

"What about a 3.0?"

"No, I said a 3.5. Do you understand, Mister?"

"Umm...yeah, I do."

"Ok. I just want to make sure we are on the same page," Loretta Lynn starts walking back to her room to search for Debra Anne's letter.

"Thanks a lot, Big Sister. Let me go call Lance and let him know." Billy Ray picks up the phone and heads to his room.

Loretta Lynn enters her room and finds the letter. She sits down and starts reading.

Dear Loretta Lynn & Billy Ray,

This is your long lost sister writing y'all today. I'm still living in New York and I'm still working as a model. I recently got married, and I have a chocolate baby girl named Samaria. I love her very much and I sometimes feel she is a payback from God. I often wonder if he put Samaria in my life, so that I can learn how to love and appreciate a human being regardless of their skin color. I adore her and wouldn't trade her in for the world. Lorretta Lynn, it has been heavy on my mind, and I want to apologize for mistreating you for so many years. I hope you can accept my apology, but I will understand if you can't. Please tell Billy Ray I said hi! I know I have never said this, but I love y'all. I have enclosed a picture of Samaria Brittney Clark.

Take Care,
Debra Anne Clark

Lorretta Lynn is staring at Samaria's picture, and tears are falling from her eyes. Samaria's picture looks identical to Lorretta Lynn's own baby picture. *Oh my, it is so funny how life works, God.* She smiles as she places Samaria's picture on her tiny nightstand. She calls out Billy Ray's name, so he can see the baby's picture. *My sister finally said she loved me. Oh, God, I bet my Grandma is in heaven smiling,* she thinks, as Billy Ray enters the room

CHAPTER NINETEEN

Billy Ray found out that he made the football team today. He's excited, and can't wait to get home to break the good news. Lorretta Lynn is on the phone with Ms. Fitzpatrick when she hears him coming in full force. She turns around to look while she's still talking. He's too excited to wait until she hangs up.

"Big Sister, I have some good news! Me and Lance made the football team," He says in a loud whisper.

"Ok, congratulations! We will talk when I get off the phone," She whispers.

"Who are you congratulating, young lady?" Ms. Fitzpatrick says.

"Oh, excuse me, Ms. Fitzpatrick. I didn't mean to be rude. Billy Ray just walked in and said he made the football team."

"Oh, that's great! Tell him I said congratulations too. That's enough to interrupt a call," Ms. Fitzpatrick says, chuckling.

"Oh, I will definitely tell him what you said, Ms. Fitzpatrick."

Lorretta Lynn and Ms. Fitzpatrick talk a while longer, and Billy Ray heads to the kitchen to eat a tuna fish sandwich. He is smiling like a Cheshire cat when Lorretta Lynn walks in.

"I'm proud of you, Baby Brother, but don't forget what I said about your G.P.A, young man."

"Oh, I won't. Trust me, I won't," He says, still smiling.

"I'm going to my room. I have a lot of studying to do," Lorretta Lynn says, with Trent and the letter she received from Debra Anne on her mind. She makes it to her room and sits down on the bed. She picks up the phone to call Trent, and then she slams it down. She pulls her book out and starts studying. A while later, she sets her book aside and begins looking through her closet. She's determined to wear a cute outfit to school. She selects some cute jeans, and a pretty sweater. As she lays her clothes out, she can hear Billy Ray talking excitedly to Lance. Feeling satisfied, she picks up her book again and resumes studying.

*****

Lorretta Lynn is sitting in her law class when Trent walks in, smelling good and looking good, as always. She's in a deep conversation with her classmate, and she's trying her best to ignore him. She glances at him while his head is facing another way. The professor has made it to class and has started the lecture. She's trying to listen attentively, but she's too preoccupied with wondering if Trent is going to approach her after class. She's looking cute, and she's wearing her hair in the style that he always liked. When class is over, Lorretta Lynn stands up quickly; she wants Trent to get a full view of her. But Trent had walked out of class without bothering to acknowledge her existence. This is her confirmation that the relationship is really over. She feels devastated, and she rushes to the bus stop.

Lorretta Lynn heads directly home from school. She often goes to the library to study on certain days, but she doesn't feel like it today. She notices Lance's bike in the front area of the apartment. For some reason she feels uneasy, because there's something about the two boys that she just can't put her finger on. She eases into the apartment and hears both boys talking. The boys appear to be in a deep conversation, and they don't hear her come in. Lorretta Lynn's inner spirit tells her to just act quiet and listen to the conversation. She hears Lance saying that he doesn't like girls. She starts listening even closer now.

"Naw, man, I really don't like girls. My mom treated my old man so bad, that she turned me against women at a young age. Nothing my dad could do was good enough for her. All she did was complain all the time. She often told him how good she look, and she could get any man she wanted. It's almost like she looked down on him because he didn't have a professional job."

"Wow, Man, that is deep. Is your mom really pretty?" Billy Ray says.

"She's not real pretty now, but a long time ago she was. You know, she's real light skinned, with long, pretty hair. She have light brown eyes, too."

"What ever happened to your dad, Man? You never talk about him."

The room is silent, and then Lance starts talking again. "Man, one day I came home from school and found my dad dead...he had committed suicide." The boys stop talking, and Lorretta Lynn can hear weeping.

Shortly after the weeping noises, she hears movements, and all of a sudden, she hears Billy Ray moaning and groaning in a joyful way. "Oh, man, it feels so good. It feels so good!"

Lorretta Lynn is in shock, and she tip toes out of the apartment. *Oh Lord, not my baby brother, oh, not my baby brother*, she thinks, as she walks around aimlessly, in a state of turmoil.

*****

Lorretta Lynn is sitting in her apartment, but her mind is a thousand miles away. Her life lately has been living Hell, and she's trying her best to just forget about all the things that have been happening. The apartment is quiet, because Billy Ray is at football practice. Her mental state is suddenly disturbed by the telephone ringing. She picks up the phone and says hello.

"Oh, hi, Lorretta Lynn, this is Ms. Fitzpatrick. How are you doing, young lady?"

"Oh, hi, Ms. Fitzpatrick, I am doing good," Lorretta Lynn lies, "how are you doing?"

"I am doing good. I know you are a busy student, but I'm calling to let you know that a relative from your Dad's side of the family is trying to get in touch with you."

"Oh, for real, Ms. Fitzpatrick? How did they get your phone number?"

"I guess your Grandmother must have given them my number and address."

"I never even met any of my Daddy's folks. My Grandma used to always say that they were bad seeds," Lorretta Lynn says, wondering why they are trying to reach her.

"Oh my. Well, I guess she felt that was the best thing to do at that time. Are you really busy right now?"

"No, I'm not busy. I'm just sitting here by myself, Ms. Fitzpatrick."

"Well, since you got some free time, I need to talk to you about something."

"Oh...ok, Ms. Fitzpatrick."

"Remember when your Grandmother made me that fruit basket?"

"Oh yes, I remember that quite well, Ms. Fitzpatrick," Lorretta Lynn says, wondering why Ms. Fitzpatrick brought this up.

"Well, I'm sure you didn't know at the time,"

"Know what, Ms. Fitzpatrick?"

"Well, she wrote a letter to me and she had it taped underneath the fruit."

"For real?"

"Yes, she did."

"What did she say on the letter, Ms. Fitzpatrick?"

"She asked me to look after you when she went home to be with the Lord. She also told me to tell you she loved you and she apologized for mistreating you over the years because of your dark skin color."

The phone is quiet now. Lorretta Lynn is thinking about all of the times she thought Hattie Mae hated her, and how badly she had been mistreated. Tears are forming, because she never dreamed that one day Ms. Fitzpatrick would be relaying an apology message from her Grandmother. First, Debra Anne apologizes and now, her deceased Grandmother's voice is coming from another human being. She stops musing and starts talking.

"Thank you so much, Ms. Fitzpatrick. I appreciate you so much. Oh my God, I just appreciate you so much. Who knows what may have happened to my life if I never met you. I thank God every day for putting you in my life," She says, and she tries to keep from breaking down.

"Oh, you are welcome, Lorretta Lynn. God put us all on this earth and we all have a purpose. My purpose just happened to be making a difference in your life. I've only done what I was called to do." Tears are in Ms. Fitzpatrick's voice.

The two talk a little longer, and Ms. Fitzpatrick says she is going to mail the letter that she received from Lorretta Lynn's relative. Not long after they hang up, Billy Ray makes it home from football practice. Lorretta Lynn is sitting in the kitchen doing homework, and Billy Ray greets her with a smile, as usual. He starts talking, and she is eager to listen.

"We had a scrimmage game today, and we won!" He says, smiling.

"Really? I thought you only had practice today. Congratulations." She replies, with a warm smile.

"Yeah, I'm pretty excited."

"Well, did you score any points?"

"No, I didn't, but my friend Lance did."

"Oh...ok." Lorretta Lynn is trying not to give away the fact that she knows what is going on between Billy Ray and Lance.

"Well, I'm tired and smelly. I am gon' go take a bath and chill. It was a tough game today."

"Oh, ok. I'm just gon' keep working on my homework."

"Is there anything good to eat in the refrigerator? I'm pretty hungry today." Billy Ray cracks the refrigerator door open.

"I guess you can open up a can of chili, like I did. Maybe you can make a chili dog, and cook some pork and beans or something."

"Pork and beans remind me of Grandma. I sure do miss her," He says, walking back to the bathroom.

"I know what you mean. I miss her, too." Lorretta Lynn is thinking about the conversation she had had with Ms. Fitzpatrick. She works on her homework for a while, and then she heads to her bedroom. Billy Ray has taken a bath, and he's in the kitchen, waiting on the chili to warm up. He's snacking on ginger snap cookies when the phone rings. He runs to the tiny living room and grabs the receiver.

"Hello."

"Hey, man, what's up?"

"Oh hey, Lance. Man, I ain't doing nothing but waiting on my chili to warm up," He says, while Lorretta Lynn is calling his name. He puts the receiver down and looks toward her room.

"Huh, Big Sister?"

"Who's on the phone?"

"Oh, it's just my friend Lance." He picks the receiver up again.

Lorretta Lynn doesn't say a word. He continues talking to Lance, while pulling the telephone cord to the kitchen. Lorretta Lynn is in her room, trying to decide if she should confront him. She thinks about it for a few minutes, and decides to just let it go.

CHAPTER TWENTY

Lorretta Lynn is on her way home from school, and stops by their mailbox. She pulls out the letter from Ms. Fitzpatrick, and dashes up to the apartment; she's anxiously anticipating what's in the letter. The apartment is quiet, because Billy Ray has not made it home. She opens the letter and starts reading.

> *Dear Lorretta Lynn Culpepper,*
>
> *This letter is to inform you that our law firm has been contacted regarding some property that you inherited from the Culpepper family. The value is very high, and we recommend that you contact our office immediately.*
>
> *Earl Stahl*
> *Law Firm*
> *318-012-4567*

Lorretta Lynn is stunned. She's nearing graduation, and she's been wondering how to pay for law school. Tears start forming in her eyes, as she reflects back to how Hattie Mae always said that the Lord will make a way. She walks to her room, holding the letter like it is a piece of gold. She pulls her twin mattress up and places the letter underneath. She picks up the phone and dials Ms. Fitzpatrick's telephone number. The phone rings about three times before Ms. Fitzpatrick picks up.

"Hello."

"Hi, Ms. Fitzpatrick. I got the letter today," Lorretta Lynn is smiling at the phone.

"Oh, you did? Was it a good news or bad news letter?"

"Actually, it was a good newsletter. I have inherited some expensive property from my Daddy's people. Now I know how I can pay for law school!"

"Oh my, Lorretta Lynn, that is excellent news! Hold on for me. Somebody is ringing my door bell. Don't hang up, my house is big, and I have to walk a little ways to the door."

"Ok, Ms. Fitzpatrick, I will hold on." Lorretta Lynn says, still smiling, and feeling on top of the world for the first time in a long time.

*****

Ms. Fitzpatrick puts the phone down, and walks downstairs to the door. She peeks out and notices her male cousin, the one who lives in another city nearby. She opens the door and lets him in. His face is red, and she's wondering what's wrong.

"Frances!" He shouts, "What is this I hear about you paying for some nigga girl education? You mean you took my Aunt's and Uncle's money, and paid for a nigga to go to school?"

"Get out my home!" Ms. Fitzpatrick screams, "Get out my home! How dare you come over here ranting and raging about my money! Get out right now, before I call the police!"

"I'm gon' get out, all right! I should take my fist and beat you to death! You ain't nothing but a nigga lover!" He's yelling, and she grabs at her heart. Ms. Fitzpatrick suddenly falls down, and her cousin starts to panic. He squats on the floor, and starts shaking her.

"Frances! Frances! Wake up! Wake up!" He says, before running to the front door and rushing outside.

*****

Lorretta Lynn is holding the phone, trying to figure out why her former teacher hasn't picked up again. Ms. Fitzpatrick's house is so big, Lorretta Lynn hears nothing but silence. She eventually hangs up the phone, thinking that Ms. Fitzpatrick was enjoying her guest and forgot she was on the phone. Billy Ray is coming in from school now. She greets him, and they start talking about his day.

Six Months Later

Lorretta Lynn is sitting in the Dean's office, waiting to be seen. She notices a guy walking in, and they catch each other's eyes briefly. He stares for a few minutes, and Lorretta Lynn starts smiling when she sees him getting ready to speak.

"Hi, my name is Derek. May I ask what is your name?"

"Oh, my name is Lorretta Lynn. Nice to meet you, Derek."

"Nice to meet you too. What brought you to the Dean's office today?"

"Oh, I just need to talk to the Dean about law school."

"Oh, really? How impressive," He says, smiling.

"Yeah, I always dreamed of becoming a lawyer. I'm gonna see what happens. What brought *you* here today? You know, one question deserves another question," She says, still smiling.

"Oh, I'm getting ready to start the MBA program and I just have some last minute questions for the Dean."

"Wow, you must be really smart. I heard the MBA program is tough, and it's hard to get into."

"Well, you know, when you have a passion for something, it makes it a little easier. I have always dreamed of owning my own company, so this is the best program for me."

"Oh, really?" She says, while the Dean is motioning for Derek to come inside his office. The Dean walks back into his office, and Derek is tearing off a piece of paper from his note pad. It has his number written on it, and she gladly accepts it when he offers. He hands her a pen, and she writes her number on his note pad. He rushes into the Dean's office, and she waits for him to come out. They wave goodbye, and she heads into the Dean's office for her appointment.

Lorretta Lynn goes home after the meeting, and Billy Ray is sitting in the living room watching T.V. They greet each other with a smile, and she starts talking.

"How was school today? Have you met a girl that you like yet, Billy Ray?"

"No, not really. A lot of girls like me, but I'm not really thinking about them. This one light skin girl, who thinks she is so pretty, is always following me around."

"How do you know that she is conceited? You might find out something different if you get to know her, Billy Ray."

"I don't want to get to know her,"

"Why not?"

"Because she remind me too much of Debra Anne."

"Boy, what I tell you about holding on to past junk?" She asks, looking at him with a serious face.

"Yeah, I remember what you said. But, I still believe that most light skin girls are stuck up, and they really turn me off," He says, without any shame.

"Boy, you are light skin yourself. Some girls might think you are stuck up," She says, with a playful smile.

"Shoot...I don't care."

"Whatever, Billy Ray. One day, you gon' eat those words. Oh yeah, I have been meaning to ask you if Ms. Fitzpatrick has called here?"

"No, she hasn't called in a long time. I was thinking maybe you had talked to her when I wasn't here."

"No, I haven't talked to her. I been trying to call, but her phone just ring and ring. I sure hope nothing has happened to her." Lorretta Lynn is still talking, when the phone rings.

"Maybe that's her now?"

"That would be nice, but..." She picks up the phone and hears Derek's voice, "Oh, hi, Derek."

"Hi. Am I speaking with Ms. Beautiful?"

"Derek, flattery gets you nowhere. How are you doing today?" She says, smiling into the phone.

"Well, I'm doing good now that I hear your voice."

Lorretta Lynn is grinning from ear to ear, and she's glad he can't see through the phone. She pulls the long telephone cord to her room and shuts the door. She doesn't want Billy Ray to hear her conversation. Billy Ray already knows she is talking to a guy, because he heard her say his name. He's glad the phone rung, because it took the heat off of him. He walks back to his room and starts working on some homework. Lorretta Lynn stays on the phone for a long time before she walks out.

"Billy Ray?"

"Yes, Big Sister?"

"Are you still keeping your grades up since football season is over?"

"Of course I am. We haven't got our report cards yet, though."

"Well, how about just showing me your school paper grades then?"

"Man, Big Sister. Are you strict or what?"

"Call it whatever you want to, Buddy."

"Ok. I hear you, Big Sister."

Some hours pass, and it is late in the afternoon. Lorretta Lynn and Billy Ray are both in their rooms, studying. Lorretta Lynn is feeling pretty good, because she spoke with her new friend today. She reads a little longer and falls asleep.

CHAPTER TWENTY-ONE

Three Days Later

Lorretta Lynn and Derek are on their first date. They decided to go to a small cafe near the school campus. Lorretta Lynn is feeling a little uncomfortable, because she and Trent had had lunch at this same cafe some months ago. She gets over her jitters and starts fumbling with the menu. Derek is looking at her with admiration written all over his face. She blushes a little when he starts talking.

"You're not nervous are you, Ms. Beautiful?"

"Oh, no, not at all. I'm just browsing through the menu trying to decide what I want."

"Well, I was checking. I know some females get nervous on their first date."

"Nah, I'm fine. This date just feels a little different," She says, smiling.

"Oh really? Is that a good thing or a bad thing?"

"Actually, it's a good thing...just feel like I have been knowing you for a long time. Kind of strange, right?"

"No, not really. You never know what might materialize," Derek says, before being disturbed by the waitress.

"Are you guys ready to place your order?" The waitress asks, her pen poised.

"Oh, I think I am ready. What about you, Beautiful?"

"I'm ready too, Derek."

"Go ahead. Ladies are supposed to go first."

"Oh, are you trying to be a gentleman today?" She says, with a playful smile.

"I'm always a gentleman, Ms. Beautiful."

She giggles, then looks at the waitress. "Oh, I think I will just take a salad and a club sandwich."

"Ok...what about you, sir?"

"Well, trust me, I sure don't want a salad. How about a deluxe cheeseburger and some chili fries?" He says, looking over at Lorretta Lynn and smiling.

The two chit chat, waiting for the waitress to bring their food. Derek is teasing Lorretta Lynn about ordering a salad. When the food arrives, the two start eating, and they act like they've known each other forever. After the meal, they head for Derek's car. When they arrive at Lorretta Lynn's apartment, Derek gets out and walks her to the door. He pecks her on the cheek and immediately walks back to his car. Lorretta Lynn walks in her apartment, and she's beaming like a spotlight. The phone starts ringing and she rushes over to pick it up.

"Hello?"

"Hi, Lorretta Lynn. This is Debra Anne."

"For real? This is my long lost sister? How are you doing, Girl? I got your letter!"

"I'm glad you got it. Were you surprised?"

"I think I was more happy than surprised. How is Samaria doing? She is absolutely adorable."

"Thank you so much, Lorretta Lynn. We are all fine. How are you and Billy Ray doing?"

"We are doing fine. He will be graduating soon, and I will be starting law school soon."

"That is so nice, Lorretta Lynn. I am proud of you guys."

"How is your modeling job coming along?"

"Oh, I'm not working right now. My husband and I decided that it would be best for me to stay home and be a full-time mom to Samaria."

"Wow, that must be a great feeling. Isn't it real expensive to live in New York?"

"Yeah, it is, but my husband is fortunate enough to have a really good job."

"Oh, really? What does he do, if I may ask?"

"Oh, yeah, no problem. He is actually head of a large engineering firm."

"Oh, well, no need to say anymore, Girl." Lorretta Lynn says, while they both chuckle.

"Yeah, I can truly say that I have been blessed with a good guy. I know we been on the phone for a while, but I need to say something before we hang up."

"I don't mind being on the phone with you. It's been so long since we even talked. You can go ahead and say what you want to say, Debra Anne."

"Oh, this is kind of hard...but it's been heavy on my mind. I have to get it out," Debra Anne hesitates. Lorretta Lynn doesn't say a word. She just holds the phone and waits for Debra Anne to talk.

"Well, I know we had a rocky relationship when we were growing up, and I'm not trying to make up any excuses, Lorretta Lynn, but I was in a lot of pain. We had lost both of our parents, and I didn't know how to deal with my feelings. You were the closest to me, so I decided to take it out on you. Grandma mistreated you, so I thought it was ok to mistreat you, too. I know I apologized in my letter, but I just want to apologize again." Debra Anne's voice is crackling, and tears are falling. Lorretta Lynn can tell that Debra Anne's being sincere, and she's just speechless. In spite of how mean Hattie Mae was, she always taught them that the Lord has a way of working things out.

"Debra Anne, I must admit that growing up with you and Grandma was very painful, but God always gave me the strength to endure. Just like he gave me the strength to endure it, he has also given me the strength to forgive y'all. Even though I didn't like your ways, I still loved you from the bottom of my heart," Lorretta Lynn says, while tears are forming in her eyes. The good thing about her tears now, is that they are happy tears. She starts wiping her tears, and Debra Anne starts talking.

"Thanks for forgiving me. This means so much to me," Debra Anne says, also wiping tears.

"You are welcome. And can you please do me a big favor?"

"Umm...sure. What type of favor do you need?"

"Oh, just give Samaria a big kiss and hug for me," Lorretta Lynn says, and they both laugh.

"That's cute. I didn't know what you were getting ready to say, Girl."

They both say "I love you" and hang up. Debra Anne feels like a heavy load has been lifted from her. She has laid in bed many nights, wondering how to apologize to her sister. She drifts back from her thoughts, and walks over to give Samaria a big kiss.

Lorretta Lynn is in a daze. She never dreamed Debra Anne would let "I love you" come out of her mouth. Hattie Mae's preaching voice is ringing in her ear: "This is another example of what God can do."

Three Years Later

Lorretta Lynn has been informed that Ms. Fitzpatrick has passed away. No one ever told her what really happened. Billy Ray is finishing his last year at a junior college. Lorretta Lynn has received a large amount of money from her inheritance, and it financed her law degree. She's presently working at a law firm, and she's engaged to Derek. Derek has completed his MBA Program, and he owns his own company. Debra Anne is still in New York, and she has a second child.

"Wow, Derek. That's a sharp convertible car you are in. Are you gon' take me for a spin?" Billy Ray says, greeting Derek at the door of their apartment.

"Man, you know I will take you for a spin anytime. Where's my beautiful fiance?"

"Oh, she's in the kitchen, cooking some good Mexican food."

"That's my girl! She knows I love Mexican food," He says, making his way to the kitchen. He turns around and starts talking to Billy Ray again, "Go ahead and get in the car. I'm gon' take you for a spin after I talk to your sis."

"Ok! I'm gon' get my cap and put some shoes on, Man."

"Alright, let me get on in this kitchen," Derek says, while Billy Ray rushes to his room.

Lorretta Lynn is in the kitchen, and he sneaks up behind her. She's stationed at the stove, and when she turns around, she's shocked to see him standing there.

"Oh my God, where did you come from? You gon' mess around and get knocked out for sneaking up on me," She says, and they greet each other with a kiss.

"Really? I'm gon' get knocked out, and you gon' get knocked up when we get married!" He says, while she playfully acts like she's getting ready to hit him.

"Well, I just wanted to holler at you. I'm getting ready to take Billy Ray for a spin in my new convertible."

"New convertible? You are lying, Derek..."

"No, I'm not. Cut the stove off for a second, and come out side and see it."

Lorretta Lynn smiles and turns the stove off. They head out of the kitchen and into the living room. She sticks her head out of the front door, and sees a silver convertible. Billy Ray is already sitting in the passenger seat. Lorretta Lynn is grinning now, and Derek is admiring her, as usual.

"Wow, Derek! You really did it up this time. I love your car."

"What do you mean, 'your car.' It's our car, Babe. We both had a challenging childhood, and I feel like we deserve this car, and some more," He says, pecking her on the cheek and walking toward the car. He turns around and starts talking before she closes the door.

"Go put the food back on. I will be ready to eat when we get back."

"Ok, Mr. Convertible," She laughs, while closing the door behind her.

Derek gets in the car and lets the top down. He takes off down the driveway, and he and Billy Ray are both wearing gigantic smiles.

Once in the kitchen, Lorretta Lynn turns the stove back on. She pulls some lettuce and tomatoes out of the fridge, and starts making a salad. This is one of the happiest times in her life, and she is loving it.

*****

Lorretta Lynn is sitting behind her desk at her small law firm job. She is looking over some files, happy that it's almost time for her to leave. The phone starts ringing, and she puts the files down. She grabs the phone and says hello.

"Hi, Lorretta Lynn, this is Henrietta. Remember, we went to law school together?"

"Hey girl, you know I remember you. How are you doing these days? I haven't heard from you in a while."

163

"I'm doing good, girl."

"How did you get my number, Henrietta?"

"Oh, I got it from one of our mutual law school friends."

"Oh, ok."

"I know we been out of touch, but I need to talk to you about a job opportunity," Henrietta's voice lowers to a whisper.

"Really?"

"Yes. But I can't talk right now. Write my number down and call me ASAP," Henrietta rattles off her number.

"You know I will, girl."

"Ok. Call me tonight around 7," Henrietta's voice is still low and mysterious.

"Ok, I will definitely give you a call. I have been meaning to get in touch with you, anyway. I want you to be one of my bridesmaids."

"Get out of here! You are getting married! Girl, I am so happy for you. Congratulations!"

"Aw, thank you, thank you."

They hang up the phone, and Lorretta Lynn is trying to figure out what kind of job Henrietta could be talking about. She looks up at the clock, and notices it is time for her to go. She finishes filing her cases, and grabs her belongings. She tells a few co-workers goodbye and exits the building. When she arrives home, she notices Derek's car in the driveway. She gets excited, and jumps out of her car. Inside the house, Billy Ray and Derek are sitting in the living room, talking.

"Hi, everybody!" Lorretta Lynn greets them with a smile.

"Hi, Ms. Beautiful. How was your day?" Derek grins at his fiance.

"Oh, I had a good day. Looks like you guys are in a deep conversation."

"Yeah, we are just talking man-to-man talk."

"Oh, really? Well, let me go to my room and pull off my work clothes. I need to talk to you about something too, Derek."

"Ok, no prob," He says, looking Lorretta Lynn up and down. Lorretta Lynn walks to her room, and he finishes his conversation.

"Well, tell me something, Man. Have you met a girlfriend at college yet?"

"Man, a girlfriend is the last thing on my mind," Billy Ray says, with a serious look on his face.

"Man, how can a guy your age not be interested in dating? I don't get it, man," Derek waits for an answer.

Billy Ray is quiet for a long minute. Finally, he starts talking again. He looks over at Derek, and Derek is waiting patiently. "Well, man, I just have to let you know that I don't do women." Billy Ray's face is as straight as a pencil.

Derek almost chokes on his soda. He looks directly at Billy Ray, "Man, what do you mean that you don't do women? Are you a virgin or something?"

"Man, it is a long story. I don't really feel like talking about it right now." Billy Ray says, looking over at Derek. The room gets quiet, and Derek is trying to make sense of what he just heard. Lorretta Lynn is in the other room, and she's talking on the phone. Derek and Billy Ray watch T.V. for a little while longer, and Derek gets up when he hears Lorretta Lynn say goodbye.

Derek leaves the living room in a confused state. He heads to Lorretta Lynn's room and peeks his head inside. Lorretta Lynn notices him looking.

"What are you doing, peeking your head in my room? Come on in, Mr. Derek."

"Oh, really?" He pushes the door open. Billy Ray clogged his mind up, so it's refreshing to be in Lorretta Lynn's presence. He refuses to inform Lorretta Lynn about the conversation that had just transpired. "What's up, babe? You mentioned that you have some good news for me?" He says, while still thinking about his talk with Billy Ray.

"Yes! My friend, Henrietta, called me at work today. She told me to call her ASAP when I got home."

"Really? Is that who you were just talking to?"

"Yeah, it was her, and guess what?"

"What, Babe?"

"She said there is a judge position where she works. She thinks I should apply."

"Really? That's awesome, Babe."

"You think so? I don't know if I have enough experience. I really haven't been out of law school that long."

"You may not have a lot of years under your belt, but you have already won a big case. People in the community are already familiar with you. I think you should apply."

"For real, Derek?"

"Yes, for real. You are very intelligent, and I think you are more than qualified to do the job," His expression is completely supportive.

"Derek, you always support me, no matter what. I really do appreciate you."

"I'm only doing what a man's supposed to do for his woman, and vice versa."

"Thank you so much, Derek!" She says, and he gives her a bear hug.

"You don't have to thank me, Babe, I know you appreciate me."

"Well, I'm a little hungry. Let me go put something on the stove."

"Ok, I'm going to go back and finish my conversation with Billy Ray."

He walks to the living room, but Billy Ray has left. Billy Ray is in his room, talking to Lance on the phone.

"Guess what, Man?" Billy Ray says.

"What, Man?"

"My sister's fiance asked me if I had a girlfriend."

"Really? Man...what did you say?"

"I told him I don't do girls."

"For real, Man? I don't know if that was a good move." Lance's voice is barely above a whisper.

"I know, Man, but he kind of caught me off guard. Before I knew it, it had already come out."

"Please don't mention my name, Man," Lance says.

"Naw, man. I would never do that."

"Thanks, Man. My pregnant wife would be devastated if she ever found out about us."

"Man, you know I would never do that to you. I love you too much," Billy Ray says, waiting on a response from Lance.

"Love you too, Dog, but I got to go. I hear my wife coming up from the basement." Lance says, rushing Billy Ray off the phone. Billy Ray puts the receiver down and he's deep in thought. He thinks back to how cruel Hattie Mae and Debra Anne were, and how he had made his mind up when he was a young boy that he didn't want to deal with girls. He prayed that over time he would have a change of heart, and that had never happened. His thoughts are disturbed by Lorretta Lynn knocking on his bedroom door.

"Billy Ray?"

"Yes, Big Sis. You can come in," He says, preoccupied with thoughts about his conversation with Lance.

"I was just checking on you. You been in here for a little while."

"Oh, I just been sitting in here talking to Lance on the phone," He says, and Lorretta Lynn starts thinking about the incident she had witnessed years ago.

"Oh, ok," She says, closing the door.

Chapter Twenty-Two

Derek has just left his business, and he's cruising over to Lorretta Lynn's. His conversation with Billy Ray has been on his mind, and he's thinking about telling Lorretta Lynn. He makes it to the house, and pulls in the driveway. He walks up to the door, and Lorretta Lynn meets him. She's talking on the phone and smiling. She whispers that she's talking to Henrietta. Derek gives her space, and starts walking around, looking for Billy Ray. Lorretta Lynn is on the phone a little while longer, and then she hangs up with more good news.

"Derek, guess what?"

"Yeah, Babe, did you get the job?" He is smiling from ear to ear.

"Not yet, but they do want me to come in for a second interview."

"Congratulations, Babe. See, I told you, you are a good candidate."

"I know, I know, we will see what happens, though."

Two Weeks Later

It's only a few days before the wedding. Lorretta Lynn went for her second interview, and she got the judge position. The hiring manager agreed to let her start after her honeymoon. Debra Anne called and said that she and her family would be attending. Some of Lorretta Lynn's distant cousins will also be coming to the wedding. Everyone is excited about Lorretta Lynn's big day, and if anybody deserves to be happy, it's definitely Lorretta Lynn.

Three Months Later

"How was work today, Baby?" Derek says, while they are sitting down to eat dinner.

"Oh, I love my job. It's very challenging, but I really love what I am doing."

"Well, I am happy for you. We both have been through some things, but it looks like our lives are finally coming together. I thank God every day that I found you, Babe."

"The same thing here. How many times in life do people really find their soul mates? We are so blessed, Derek."

"Yes, I would have to agree with you, one hundred percent. When is your next trial, Baby?"

"Oh, it's actually this week."

"Is it a big one? I guess all trials are big, though," He says, while they both get up from the dinner table. They put their plates in the sink and walk to the living room. They watch movies for a long time, and then they crash.

*****

Derek is sitting in his office when he gets a call from Lorretta Lynn. He can tell by her voice that she's in distress. *Oh my, what has happened to my wife?*

"Derek! Derek! Meet me at the restaurant, down the street from my job!" Lorretta Lynn is sobbing into the phone.

"What's wrong? What's wrong? Talk to me, Lorretta Lynn!"

"I can't talk right now! I can't talk! Please, just jump in your car and come as fast as you can!" She says, before slamming down the phone.

Lorretta Lynn rushes out of the courthouse's side door, and Derek rushes out of his business. Derek jumps in the convertible, and he's driving like a cop on a high speed chase. Lorretta Lynn is shaking and crying as she's fumbling to get her car door open. She finally gets it open and jumps in the car. She puts her foot on the accelerator, and speeds out of the courthouse parking lot. Visitors are looking, trying to figure out what's going on. Before they know it, she is totally out of sight. When she makes it to the restaurant, she is crying hysterically. Derek pulls up, looking like a mad man. He parks his car and jumps out. He rushes over to her vehicle, and sees that she is hysterical.

"Lorretta Lynn! Lorretta Lynn! Tell me what happened to you at work!" Derek jumps in through her passenger door.

"Calm down, Baby, calm down." He reaches over and caresses her.

"Oh, Derek, I had such a horrible day at work," She says, trying to calm down a little.

"I'm here now, Baby, I'm here. Go ahead and talk to me," He says, in a low and husky masculine tone.

"Well, I was sitting in my judge's seat, reviewing a case file at the last minute..."

"And?"

"I was reading about an elderly man who had been sexually molesting little girls," Lorretta Lynn is just bawling.

Derek is confused, because he knows this is part of her job. His head is pounding, and he can't make sense of what is going on. He caresses her even harder, and says, "Spit it out, Baby, just spit it out."

"When I looked up at the client, I noticed it was the fruit man who brutally raped me when I was a teenage girl," Lorretta Lynn gets the words out before breaking down and shaking.

"Ahh, Baby, ahh Baby, I'm so sorry to hear that." He holds her and tells her that everything is going to be ok. He looks in her red, bloodshot eyes, and asks, 'What did you do when you realized it was him, Baby?"

"I got up from my judge's chair, and rushed back to where Henrietta was; I told her I couldn't conduct the trial because the client was the man that brutally raped me when I was a teenager. Henrietta turned red and told me to leave. She said she was going to make sure that he never sees the outside world again. She rushed in the courtroom and sat where I was sitting. I'm assuming she sentenced him to life in prison."

"Oh my, what a long day, Baby. What a long day. Let's just leave your car here. We'll come back and pick it up tomorrow. Let's go home. I'm going to make up for everything that happened today. I feel like getting my shotgun...oh, I feel like getting my shotgun."

"God is our shotgun, Derek. He gon' take care of him." Lorretta Lynn says, while Derek is pulling out of the restaurant parking lot. If Derek didn't know the Lord, he probably would have gone to jail for the things he wanted to do. The car is silent now, and Lorretta Lynn is resting her head on Derek's shoulder. *God, it was a terrible day and it was a good day. The man that tortured my body and mind will finally be locked up. Justice has finally been served!* Derek pops some love songs into the radio, and guides the car down the long, busy city street.

Two Years Later
Lorretta Lynn and Derek have twin girls now. They purchased a five bedroom home in the suburbs. Lorretta Lynn is still working as a judge, and Derek has acquired a second company. Billy Ray has come out of the closet, and Lorretta Lynn and Derek have accepted his sexuality and lifestyle. Lorretta Lynn's family and Debra Anne's family have become very close. Billy Ray has found happiness, working as a chef at a major hotel.

DISCUSSION QUESTIONS

1. Do you think dark skinned people are still treated differently?
2. Do you think people like "Ms. Fitzpatrick" really exist?
3. Do you think grandparents show favoritism towards the grandkids they feel are prettier?
4. Do you think the racism issue is better, worse, or the same?
5. Do you think it is the parent's responsibility, to educate kids regarding race relations?
6. Do you think it will ever be a time, when the majority will love people regardless of their origin or nationality?
7. What did you take away from this story?
8. What is a good rating for this book? (1 thru 5)

ABOUT THE AUTHOR

Gloria G. Williams is a native of Saginaw, Michigan. She has been writing for almost 21 years. Her first book was published in 2005 (*Wow! Poetry*). She was offered a record deal contract and declined due to undisclosed reasons. She has also won awards for poetry. In addition, Gloria received an associate degree from Delta Community College. After graduating from Delta, she continued her education at Eastern Michigan University. Soon after graduation, she was accepted into a non-degree Graduate Sociology intern program at Wayne State University. She worked in the field of social work for several years and then decided to move on to a Fortune 500 company. She enjoys spending quality time with family and close friends.